Galloper's Quests

The Fall of Earth and the Rise of a New Destiny

Augustus Cileone

Prologue

Original Letter to the Publisher

I'm back where I started. I escaped my jail on Earth and returned only to find myself in a cell once again. All I wanted was to help my fellow humans by sharing my experiences. But my government considers me a criminal and a security risk, and I am again isolated. I feel the walls of this place pressing in on me. Through my one window I am not able to see beyond the walls surrounding the facility, which makes me yearn for the view of the infinite I once experienced among the stars. Even worse, the one I brought back with me, for whom I care very much, has also lost her freedom. Through my brother, Arthur, who is your client, I have been able to smuggle this digital copy of my story based on my log entries that recorded my adventures. I thank you in advance for reading my tale and hope you have the courage to inform the public of what it reveals. I must admit that my faith in humanity following my wartime experiences has lapsed and any effort to obtain true insights may be pointless. But maybe our people are capable of learning from the lives of others, no matter how strange they may seem.

Captain Samuel Galloper, USN

Part One

Burc

Chapter One

I am looking at the vastness of space and I feel both liberated and frightened at the same time. Through the viewer of my ship, the Seeker, Earth is no longer in sight. I am not sure what is to become of me, but I felt compelled to break away from what was happening. I will record this log for myself and possibly for others, if it turns out to be of any worth.

My name is Samuel Galloper. I am a captain in the U. S. Navy. My grandfather and father were military men, and I felt the need to carry on the tradition. I am also a scientist. These two aspects of myself often collided inside of me and with others. One part of me never questions, the other is always questioning.

The scientist in me invented a propulsion system made for interstellar travel. The Seeker was not meant to go on a distant voyage at this point. Its first flight was supposed to be a mechanical dress rehearsal to try out all the parts to see if everything came into play as it should. The official plan was for the craft to spend nine months circling Mother Earth, testing the propulsion system by doing split-second runs. That was the mission the military assigned me to carry out. That was what a soldier did. To do otherwise, to think for myself, to make my own decisions, would lead to chaos. But, ironically, the Navy had given me a great deal of time to think, and I thought about why I should question what others told me to do.

One individual I came in conflict with was Admiral Victor Rutlaw. I became a pilot twenty years ago, when I was twenty-one, in a fleet commanded by Rutlaw during the Turkish War in 2059. Russia tried to conquer Turkey, a NATO member, and the United States had to uphold its agreement to defend treaty members. The Admiral seemed obsessive about aggressively attacking the enemy, even when opposing troops were retreating. He would whip up his men into a patriotic frenzy before each assault.

The conflict dragged on for five years. Weapons from both sides killed many people and devastated the land. The conflict ended with a split Turkey, one part in NATO and the other under Russian rule. I witnessed my fill of human devastation during that time.

I became wary of how the military would use my propulsion invention when NASA assigned Admiral Rutlaw as the new project manager. I became alarmed as I knew that he supervised the development of weapons under the Defense Department. He persistently questioned me about my research.

"How large an object could your invention transport?" he asked one time, barging in on me while I was working with robotic assembly of my propulsion system.

"I haven't configured anything greater than the size of the test spacecraft," I said, trying to put him off at least for a while.

"What about the number of military personnel? How many people at one time?" he said.

"Again, it would depend on the size of the transport," I said.

"Well can't you tell me how many would fit inside the Seeker? And suppose we had numerous vehicles the size of the Seeker? Can't you extrapolate from that? You're the smart scientist after all."

"We're still in the developmental stage. I will inform you of confirmed successful findings. There will be no transporting if I don't get back to work," I said, and I turned away from Rutlaw, signaling the end of the conversation.

"We're done for now," he said before leaving. "But I'll want answers, and I mean soon."

I tried going over Rutlaw's head by talking to the NASA chief, Director Ernest Wizend, who, like me, was a war veteran who joined the space program.

"Sir, shouldn't we share my findings with the world?" I asked Wizend in the middle of my project. "If the scientists of the planet worked together as a community, we may be able to speed up our progress."

"I know you realize, as a military man," said the Director, "that information about your invention could be used by enemies against the United States. I appreciate your caution, Sam, as we both know how scientific breakthroughs can turn into horrifying weapons. But the threat of enemy nations or terrorists obtaining your findings can be devastating. We must prevent that possibility from ever happening."

I knew if I openly rebelled, the military might take my work out of my hands. So, I tried to sidestep Rutlaw.

"Can I continue to convey all of my findings to the Space Exploration Branch?" I asked.

"I'm sorry," said Wizend. "The President said that Rutlaw was the only person you are to report to."

I saw that the links of the chain of command held firm, and I knew I could not bend their iron rule.

Chapter Two

My older brother, Arthur, who is an author of speculative fiction, knew about my desire to make space travel faster. My relationship with my brother has always been a close one, even if we disagreed many times on the extent of my scientific zeal. He visited me as often as possible from his home in Towson, Maryland. However, NASA would not allow me to reveal the details of my work to him because of security reasons, and I missed talking with him about my project.

"How are you doing, cooped up in here," Arhtur asked on one visit where we met for some coffee in the cafeteria of the NASA Development and Integration Command Center in Greenbelt, Maryland. "I know how much you dislike being confined. That time you got stuck in an elevator when you were twelve freaked you out."

"Yeah, I still prefer taking the stairs, if possible," I said.

"You taking some down time?" he asked. "All work and no play make Sam a pain in the ass."

"You're the butt ache," I said. "I enjoy working."

"I don't know," said Arthur. "It's like a fever with you. You need to cool down sometimes or that big brain of yours will overheat. Maybe keep reading those books I recommended."

I wanted to confide in Arthur about what I was going through. How excited I was participating in such a monumental project, but also how frightened I was if I couldn't have a say in the use of my invention. The reality was I had to keep my thoughts to myself since I was ordered to do so.

***

When the Admiral became frustrated with my slow progress, he transferred me to the NASA base in Florida which was a more remote and secure location. The building had numerous sections that were cut off from each other for security control. There were hardly any windows in the inner part of the building which aggravated my claustrophobia. Rutlaw was able to confine me to the building since it had living accommodations on site. He justified all of the restrictions on the rationale of maintaining the confidentiality of the mission. Rutlaw probably did not want me to do an end-around-run by leaking my findings to the rest of the world which he felt would undermine American superiority in the international weapons race. He put me under constant surveillance. The military intelligence officers screened all my communications. I was not allowed to speak with visitors alone.

I had a meeting with Rutlaw and Admiral Rockford Moreland of the Joint Chiefs to address my concerns about the project. It was like running into a brick wall.

"I hope that my work will be used for peaceful purposes," I said.

"Must I remind you of your patriotic duty as an officer in the U.S. Navy?" said Rutlaw. his jutting jaw pointing at me. "You do not give orders, you carry them out,".

"You have been provided abundant funding and support to make your project become a reality," Moreland said as he looked over an appropriations screen on his tablet.

I had seen this day coming.

"I would like to suggest that I be the one to command the Seeker alone so that no one else will be in danger if the experiment fails," I said. "For security reasons, personnel should be kept to a minimum, and each person's knowledge will be restricted to her or his own tasks. I'll use computers, 3-D printers, and robotics to complete the construction and installation of the propulsion system. If the project is a success, I'll supervise the military briefing concerning all the scientific specifications and data."

After much debate, Rutlaw and Moreland agreed to the proposal.

So, I had my orders. But, I could not let the military transform my hopeful ideas into deadly realities, even if it meant leaving my home behind.

Rutlaw didn't trust me about sharing information, so he tried to subvert any autonomy I maintained on the project by placing tech spies to work with me to acquire intelligence for him. One of them was Dr. Frank Amico. I found out that we both went to MIT, but he graduated a few years before me. We also shared a love of classic science fiction films, like *Forbidden Planet* and *The Day the Earth Stood Still*.

"What did you major in?" Frank asked me while I was working with some robotic facilitators.

"I double-majored in astrophysics and philosophy. Turns out I had an aptitude for both disciplines," I said.

"That's an interesting contrast," Frank said.

"Yeah, but science was my primary occupation. I excelled in science and mathematics when I was young. Graduated high school at the age of fourteen and undergrad studies at sixteen. I became obsessed with space exploration. I studied satellite and manned explorations in the solar system. I eventually worked as an astrophysicist for NASA. Wizend became interested in my theories about the mechanics needed to achieve interstellar exploration of the cosmos, and he supported my research. I guess you already know I focused on trying to find a way to travel great distances in short periods of time so that we could explore deep space."

"Why space travel?" he asked.

"I believe humans could not hope to acquire and fit together the parts of the whole that made up the story of existence without exploring the universe."

"I can see where the philosophy major plays a part here," said Frank with a chuckle. "I was strictly a computer guy, mainly security systems. I wanted to help protect our country from cyber-attacks."

"So, you're a patriot?" I asked, trying to gauge his commitment to Rutlaw.

He thought for a minute, and then said, "Yeah, sure. Although I'm not always comfortable with some of my country's actions."

"Like what?" I said.

Frank looked around and said in a whisper, "Some algorithms I created for defensive purposes Rutlaw adapted to attack other countries. Sometimes indiscriminately. He targeted fuel, sanitation, and medical infrastructure which made innocent civilians victims."

"Then why cooperate with Rutlaw?" I asked.

"Rutlaw wasn't always like this," he said. "He used to be a prisoner exchange negotiator. He was quite successful in getting military and civilian releases from several countries. One of those was my brother Walter, a journalist. He was in China, reporting on rumors about chemical warfare development. That's why I went to work for Rutlaw. But then, some Middle Eastern terrorists betrayed him on a deal to release captured American travelers, including children, held for ransom. They beheaded the captives. It shook him badly. He asked for a leave of absence. When he returned to duty he seemed calm on the outside, and I continued to work with him. But I realize now he doesn't trust anybody, especially foreigners."

I found as I worked with Frank that I could confide in him and hoped to enlist him as an ally. He became curious about my propulsion system.

"I originally wanted to develop a harmonic matter-wave propulsion system which could convert a human and a spacecraft into electromagnetic energy and transport them at the speed of light. It sounded like a crazy science fiction proposal. However, after several years of scientific gestation I was able to deliver conclusive results that grew from my idea."

"That does sound like sci fi becoming science fact," said Frank.

"I know, but the more I worked on it," I said, "I realized the system had the capability to propel a spacecraft thousands of light years in a few minutes. I call my invention the HOPS, the Harmonic Operation Propulsion System. If I entered the proper settings, the HOPS would use the electromagnetic energy derived from photons which are created from electrons dropping to lower orbits. Photons are little parcels of energy. My system uses a transducer, a cylindrical unit, that is essential to the wave/matter conversion, and without which the HOPS could not connect the craft to a cosmic continuum, folding space, and, in effect, creating its own wormhole. I also also added cooling element that will attract "exotic matter" which repels gravity to keep the wormhole open during transport."

Frank rubbed his face and said, "You're way over my head on all of this stuff."

"Okay," I said, knowing Frank loved the *Back to the Future* films. "Just think of the transducer as my "flux capacitor."

I paused before continuing.

"I haven't told Rutlaw about the above or what I'm about to tell you now. It's a bit frightening. It is possible that my invention could reverse the transformation of matter to electromagnetic energy and reduce objects in reconversion to various states of density, theoretically to the point of forming a black hole, sucking everything into a cosmic point of immense gravity."

Frank let out a hiss of air through his lips.

"I can see why you withheld that info," he said. "In the wrong hands that could be devastating."

"I am afraid that now that the military has commandeered my work, I'm worried that they will pervert my invention for their own purposes," I said. "Will you help me, Frank? I know I'm asking a lot of you."

Frank thought it over briefly and said, "What do you want me to do?"

Chapter Three

As the launch of the Seeker drew closer, I asked Frank if he could program encrypted deletion software into the computer servers remotely that would ensure that nobody could reproduce my work on the propulsion system. I still was nervous about being found out during the process, and I also worried about what would happen to Frank.

"I appreciate your concern," said Frank. "But I can do this since I devised the security systems here. Programmers insert backdoors that they use to get back into a system if they have to bypass safeguards so they can fix bugs. I can insert the deletion malware."

"You'll be the first one who will be suspected," I said. "I don't like that you are taking such a risk."

"I will make it look like the cyber-attack occurred from some foreign country, like North Korea," he said. "Also, I've been looking to get out of this gig anyway. I will disappear and create a new identity elsewhere. Always wanted to live on Sardinia."

After several more months my work was completed. It was springtime and the launch of the Seeker was set. Frank was ready to wipe my work after I took off. Days before I was to take off I started to get cold feet. I was still a military man, and I started to feel like a traitor to my country, which had helped me in bringing my mental creation into physical existence. I pictured my crew-cut, muscular father, who, despite pledging his allegiance to the need for discipline in the ranks, was an understanding person, who observed my intellectual restlessness, and provided me safety in the routines he developed in the service. He was a Navy man, though, and just like him I was drawn to the ocean, that seemingly limitless stretch of water waiting for me to explore it. I loved playing the navigator on my father's boat, steering the craft, riding the crests, and laying in courses. The oceans connected all of us to each other. So, I kept reminding myself I had a responsibility to the world as a whole and did not want to contribute to humanity's drive toward self-destruction.

The liftoff was flawless. I felt as if I was experiencing a rebirth, straining to free myself from Mother Earth's gravitational hold. During numerous orbits, I took time to ensure that the life-support systems, warning signals, and structural integrity of the spacecraft remained within acceptable operating parameters. At the designated time for the first initiation of the harmonic drive I began to disconnect all readings that automatically monitored the ship from Mission Control. At this predetermined time, Frank initiated a remote reformatting of all computer drives on the ground and activated viruses that wiped out my data on any files associated with the project that were in the military cloud storage. As soon as these actions reached Rutlaw's attention he became incensed.

"Galloper, this is Admiral Rutlaw. What the hell is wrong with you? What kind of treasonous act are you trying to pull?"

"Well, well. If it isn't admirable Admiral Rutlaw," I said. "Have they sent you to tell me to ship up or ship out?"

"What's the matter with you, Galloper?" said Rutlaw, amping up the volume of his voice. "You are sabotaging your mission, man!"

"I know," I said. I knew what I had to do.

"We don't know what's going on with you, soldier. Somehow you've destroyed the data for this project. You're disgracing your uniform, Galloper. You deactivated the biological readings so we can't tell if your actions are due to some sort of physical or mental condition."

"I can tell you what's happening, Admiral. I'm cutting the cord. This baby is on its own, now."

"You're acting like a big baby, Galloper. Stop this bullshit!"

"I'm going to do a little talking and you are going to do a little listening for a change," I said.

I paused to suck on my hydration tube.

"I was content being a Navy man for quite a while. Life on board a ship suited me. Military life gave me a direction, kept me busy. There was no time for questions. You had your job and you did it, knowing you were one small cog in a vast machine. But, there was also the sea and the sky, those seemingly borderless stretches before me. It tempered the set, limited life of a soldier with a sense of the infinite."

I sounded almost nostalgic, but only for a moment.

"Then the war came. I found myself serving under your command, Admiral. I saw infernal sights: blood red; limbs torn; bodies bursting in air. The weapons of war were unfeeling and relentless, mirroring what their makers had become. I found myself staring down often into the depths of the ocean, trembling at the horror of the human urge for violence. After my father died as a pilot in that war, I started to hate the military for birthing its lethal creations."

I took another sip of water, and for a split-second my body started to shake as I wondered what it would be like if my invention failed, and I could not drink or eat again.

"My sympathies began to lie less with the ship and more with the vastness surrounding it. I decided to apply my talents to setting sail on the ultimate sea - space. I thought the rigorous training program would do me some good, and it did, for a while. But the more I feared the military's destructive mentality, I began to despise minds that thought like yours did."

I could hear Rutlaw's breathing, which had become more rapid as I spoke.

"Okay, mister." said Rutlaw after he took a deep breath, and I knew he was trying to restrain his anger. "Because of the seriousness of the present situation, we're going to forget what you've just said. Now that you've got things off your chest, maybe you'll get back to doing your job. Things will go better for you if you just follow orders. We contacted your brother in Maryland and gave him access to this communication. He wants to talk to you."

I closed the audio channel. The light began to blink again, and I could imagine the troubled and confused look on Arthur's face at the other end of the link. He didn't even know the truth about the flight. The press release stated that NASA was testing a new unmanned rocket engine along with weather information gathering equipment. I stared at the pulsing red light, throbbing like a vein on a frightened animal. I decided to turn the switch back on.

"Come in Seeker. Seeker, come in!"

I was silent.

"Sam, it's Arthur."

"Arthur. It's April again. April is the cruelest month, Arthur. It makes thoughts, which were better left buried, break through to the surface, and thrusts them into the light of day."

"Sam, I'm worried about you. You know you must cooperate now so you can be safe."

I ignored my brother's deep, soothing voice. It had an almost hypnotic tone, and I was determined to resist its effect.

"Arthur, you know what I've been doing? Going around in circles. I have been whirling around the planet, not getting anywhere. Life is a loop for most people. And the moon goes around the earth, and the earth spins on its axis, and the earth goes around the sun, and there's nothing new under the sun, Arthur. There isn't any progress, brother. There are no meaningful breakthroughs. No desire to truly find what existence is all about."

"Sam, please," said Arthur, and I could almost see tears forming in his eyes. But I wouldn't let my train of thought be derailed.

There was a brief silence. Then Arthur began to speak again in a monotone, as if he had surrendered to an inevitability.

"I thought that the books I gave you would help. I thought they would show you how other minds dealt with life's questions."

"They were just more material added to build a labyrinth inside me, with a minotaur asking the gnawing question ... 'Why?'"

I stopped for a few seconds.

"Goodbye, Arthur."

"Sam! Don't! Come back to me!"

I secured myself in the pilot's seat. I switched off the computer's guidance system, and I took manual control. I heard the hurried exchange between Arthur and Rutlaw.

"What's going on?" said Arthur.

"He's switched over to manual," said Rutlaw. "Now listen here, Galloper. You better start obeying orders ..."

I inhaled deeply and then ignited the thruster engines.

"What the hell are you doing, Galloper!" screamed Rutlaw.

"What's happening?" said Arthur.

"He's taking the ship out of orbit. Come in, Seeker!"

I closed the communications link. As the ship broke loose from earth's gravitational pull, I felt untethered. I was truly alone now. I leaned forward to stare out of the viewing window as the ship soared into the endless void. I sank back into the seat, continued to gaze, and began to think.

Chapter Four

Loneliness began to close in on me as I put distance between myself and my world. That umbilical connection is difficult to cut, but I made a commitment to the severing, and now had to take responsibility for my actions.

The Seeker was a sleek craft, looking like a cross between the old space shuttles and the aerodynamic design of a Chevrolet Corvette. As Doc Brown says in *Back to the Future*, if you're going to design a mode of transport, you should do it with some "style." The inside, despite all the technical gear, was comfortably roomy, with a space for sleeping in the form of an enclosed hammock. There were also secured food and liquid storage bins, toiletry facilities, digital library (including music and films), medical supplies, and closets of clothes to free me from my cumbersome spacesuit.

There were strict guidelines to observe regarding the HOPS. After each metamorphosis there needed to be a thirty-four-hour wait period before the next conversion so that the solid nature of the ship and its occupants could stabilize. If the reconversion to the wave state took place within too short a time period, or if the return to the matter stage did not take place within the thirty-four-hour parameter, the ship and those inside it would accelerate in the form of electromagnetic waves, and dissipate into infinity. The return to a solid state needed to be precisely concluded or else the atomic structure of the ship and its occupants would continue to contract into a dense vortex if there was no termination of the process sooner. In that case an immense gravitational abyss would emerge which could suck a planet the size of Earth into its destructive center.

My intention was to visit various parts of the galaxy and seek out other life forms. If my supplies ran out before finding an inhabitable planet, I decided I would not return to Earth. My home planet had its chance of retaining me as an inhabitant, but its violent members showed no sign of ending their murderous ways. Instead, I planned to transition into the wave state and not reconvert, allowing me to join with the infinite.

I laid in a course for the Dopple I system where deep space probes had indicated there was the possibility that life existed on planets there based on atmospheric conditions and the presence of water. I set a countdown to initiate the HOPS to the setting where it would create the wormhole effect.

What I experienced was shattering. When the device activated, there was intense vibrating and a visual blurring of the inside of the Seeker. The perception of objects losing their shape was terrifying at first. There was then the sense of the craft and me along with it becoming compressed and then sucked with extreme speed into an illuminated funnel-like stream of movement. It felt like I was losing my body's physical integrity. My short, dark beard stretched out in front of me and my wavy brown hair seemed to trail behind my head. I became disoriented and frightened as I began to envision numerous images: babies being born; soldiers dying; families enjoying dinner together; bodies being dumped into mass graves; paintings by Vincent Van Gogh; the Egyptian pyramids; the buildings of Hiroshima blasted away. I saw myself holding a white book with a black question mark on its cover. Just as I was about to reveal the book's contents, I lost consciousness.

I awoke, which was a surprise in itself. I was excited by the fact that my propulsion system that sprung from my scientific imagination, like Athena from Zeus's brain, had worked as I had envisioned. I reviewed the Seeker's systems and found they were functioning properly. I was almost afraid to check my vital signs. I was relieved to see that my blood pressure and pulse were only slightly elevated, despite the fact that during the jump it felt as if my heart was going to explode.

I turned on the external viewer and saw that I was approaching a planet about a third larger than the size of earth. I increased the magnification and was excited to see that there were pockets of what appeared to be manufactured structures in various locations. There were also large areas that showed no such construction. I was amazed that my calculations had brought me so close to an inhabited planet. The significance of the moment paralyzed me for several minutes.

I reanimated myself to note that the gravity of the planet was increasing the speed of the Seeker, pulling it toward the surface like a fish snared on a hook. The sensors detected an atmosphere. I let the guidance computer position the craft so that its heat shields on the bottom of the ship would protect it from burning up as the automatic pilot maneuvered the craft toward a landing site. I then assumed manual control of the Seeker and navigated it toward one spot that appeared to be barren. I landed behind a plateau rock formation. I wanted to avoid a dramatic confrontation with any local inhabitants, if there were any still in existence, that might provoke fear and retaliation.

After I landed, I took readings and found that the atmosphere was similar to that of earth, but the oxygen level was a bit thinner which would require restriction of prolonged labor.

The temperature was equivalent to what occurred during autumn in the eastern part of the United States. I was relieved that I was able to remove my outer spacesuit. I gathered food consisting of mineral and vitamin enriched protein bars, and water stored aboard the Seeker. I stowed them in an exploratory backpack that I swung onto my shoulders. I unlocked the hatch and exited the sanctuary of the Seeker, feeling wary but also exhilarated, on the road to discovering a new world. Perhaps I would find inhabitants here that would be open to looking for answers to the universe's mysteries. However, I did not want to be foolish. My dad always told me to prepare for exploring new places by being cautionary. So, I tempered my enthusiasm with wariness. I removed the transducer device and buried it not far from the Seeker. It had a tracking chip on it, and I would be able to find it again with a setting on my wristwatch that acted like a GPS. I had a tiny digital video/audio recorder that was suspended from a chain which I wore around my neck. It contained a high-capacity memory chip so I could continue to record my log.

The sky was covered in thick, dark clouds that appeared to have pock marks in them. They made me think of saturated sponges waiting to release their moisture. Indeed, it did start to rain while I walked. There was a damp, almost oppressive smell in the atmosphere. The increased gravity slowed me down. I saw that even though I had good musculature, my legs were not strong enough for extended movement. I would have to take several breaks before I could reach an inhabited area. As I continued to walk, I observed that along with natural stone structures, there were also large areas of mud. To test the safety of the path I gathered rocks and threw them around me. Some sank quickly indicating that the ground in some places was like quicksand. As I proceeded, I came across some large craters. I wondered if these were due to meteorites, but then I passed by one that seemed to be still in the process of forming. I deduced that the topography produced sinkholes, and that I ought to be careful as I approached where I had observed there may be inhabitants.

After walking a few miles, dodging several spots that I deemed hazardous, I saw a settlement that was visible through a large opening in a stone wall. I hid behind an outcropping of rock and pulled out my viewing scope to get a closer look. What I witnessed seemed like a contradiction in technology. There was a tall, pyramid-shaped building in the middle of the community whose surface looked smooth and modern. There were metallic robotic sentries, also triangular in shape, with claw-like hands, scattered about, that seemed to be observing the area. The planet's inhabitants were tearing down rudimentary wood and concrete structures with implements that resembled axes and clubs. Others used tools similar to hammers, screwdrivers, and cement, as they repaired the fronts of structures that others just destroyed along the center road of the community. I witnessed several of the workers digging holes in the ground, and others illogically filling up the openings that the others had just dug. These actions were very confusing to me.

These beings were humanoid, but there were significant differences from Earth's inhabitants. The heads were smaller than those of people on my planet and the bodies larger and squatter. They appeared to be wearing several layers of clothing. I noticed a shimmer as some sunlight caught the face of one. I zoomed in and saw crystals, also in the form of triangles, embedded on each temple which glowed dimly. The soldier in me was alert for any sign of violence even from what appeared to be unarmed inhabitants. But, I also felt excited as I was discovering something new.

Since I did not wish to initiate fear in these individuals, I decided to slowly approach this community with my hands raised to show I was not a threat. When I reached a couple of the workers, they dropped their implements and stared. The crystals on their heads began to blaze brightly. Almost immediately an alarm went off. The robotic guards whisked away those who became aware of my presence. Two of the sentries leaped to my side and used their metallic appendages to secure me. I began to protest and another of their kind covered the upper part of my body with a dark sack. As the alarm ceased, they picked me up as if I were weightless and I was rushed away, unseen and unseeing.

Chapter Five

I could tell that the synthetic sentries took me inside a building since it became quieter in the space where we came to a halt. One of the robots forced me to sit in a chair and removed the sack that covered me. The robot retreated to a door where it stood sentry with the other of its kind on either side of the portal, which was narrower at the top compared to the middle of the aperture. They became completely still, appearing unaware of my presence. Their surfaces consisted of a black metal and their triangular form was consistent with the humanoids, having smaller head components compared to the rest of their shape. I saw that I was in a large room with dark metallic walls. There was a wide desk in front of me that appeared to be made of some sort of stone whose markings reminded me of granite. There were many viewing screens behind the desk that displayed inhabitants doing a variety of activities. I heard a whooshing sound to the left side of my chair, and a black door, shaped like the other opening (which I was to discover mimicked all doorways on the planet) slid open. The individual who passed through the aperture had a larger head than the others I had seen, but it still was smaller than an average human one. Instead of draping himself in a variety of clothing, the individual wore only a flowing gray robe. Even more interesting was that he had no crystals on his forehead. He was shorter than my five-foot, ten-inch height by about three inches, yet he was taller than the other inhabitants I had seen. I theorized that the strong gravitational force of the planet was instrumental in limiting the height of the individuals here.

I assumed the being to be a male of the species because he had a short, dark gray beard, not unlike my own, and similar wavy hair on his head. In contrast, I had observed an inhabitant prior to my capture who had no hair on the face and appeared to be pregnant. I saw others I took for females because they had curves under their clothing that suggested that they had breasts and wider hips than the others. Besides the difference in the head and body size, the inhabitant in front of me had facial features similar to humans. His bright gray eyes were particularly welcoming.

He barked some monosyllabic grunts at the robots who left after receiving their commands. The alien then came closer and scrutinized me from head to toe. He then began to circle me. I stayed alert, not knowing what to expect. After he completed his orbital surveillance, he pointed to the desk and uttered the monosyllable "ry." He repeated the gesture and the sound. Assuming he was telling me his word for "desk," I repeated the sound as best as I could. He then rewarded me with a smile, which was reassuringly human. He then used one hand to point to me, and his other indicated the desk. I deduced he wanted my word for the object, and I said "desk." He then repeated "desk," and seemed pleased with the sound he produced. I felt relieved by the attempt to communicate on the part of someone who seemed to be an important individual of this civilization.

He then pointed to himself and said, "Lask," which I gathered was the being's name. I repeated "Lask," and received another smile. I reciprocated by pointing to myself and announced, "Sam," since I concluded that my single-syllable nickname would work best in this place. Once again, my host rewarded me with a smile. Lask then used his hands to imitate eating and drinking. I said "eat" and "drink," and Lask looked encouraged with the sounds of the words. He raised an arm and beckoned me to follow him. He pushed a button on the wall which slid open the door through which he entered, and we passed through the opening. The room we entered was more rustic, with no electronic equipment. The windows were in the form of triangles. There was a large triangular-shaped table in the middle of it that looked like it was made of dark, heavy wood. The chairs consisted of the same material and the backs were wide at the base and tapered upward to a point. There were plates on the table which mimicked the triangular geometric form, and the drinking goblets next to the plates had stems on which sat conical vessels that had smaller openings at the top.

Lask motioned for me to sit down in front of one of the silvery metal drinking cups and a plate, which seemed to be made of a sort of clay. He sat next to me and took what I guessed were meat and vegetables from a large serving dish onto his plate. He then poured some clear liquid into his goblet and mine. There was only one type of eating instrument available, which was made of dark metal, and it had a handle attached to a three-sided base which tapered to a point. My host obviously was willing to trust me based on my nonviolent behavior thus far since he allowed me to hold an object that could be used as a weapon. I was encouraged by this accommodation. Lask used his dining instrument to jab a bit of the meat and took a bite. He then sipped his beverage. He gestured for me to partake. I assumed his preliminary actions were to alleviate any fears I might have that the food and drink could be harmful to me. The increased gravity tired me, and I felt the need for sustenance. Yet I still was wary of the effect the alien nourishment might have on my earthly digestive system. I decided to give it a try since dehydration and starvation were not an option. The food had a charcoal smell, so I assume it was roasted. I found it filling, consisting of some type of fowl, and no, it did not taste like chicken. It was more gamey. There were root vegetables that were chewy. I never liked overly seasoned or spicy food, but this dinner was particularly bland. The liquid had the same properties as water on earth, only it tasted a little sweet. The food smelled a bit burnt, but there was no charred taste.

Apparently the way that I devoured the cooked bird displeased Lask. I began with the breast and was going to proceed to the wings and then the legs. Lask tapped me, shook his head, and showed me that I should reverse the order. I shrugged to imply it did not matter, but Lask seemed disturbed by my response. I decided I did not want to upset a potentially powerful ally on this planet, so I conformed to his instructions.

I had not finished my meal when a low-pitched alarm emanated from what I had noticed was a slowly rotating triangular dial on the wall. Robots entered the room and quickly removed the food and plates. I assumed that the wall dial was a timer and that it signaled that the eating time was over. Lask gestured to have me follow him. He led me through another door into an adjoining chamber that was a combination bedroom/study. It had a triangular bed against a stone wall. There were dark wood bookcases on another wall with bound reading material. The viewing screen sitting on a granite-like desk added to the contrasting modern and rudimentary elements of the room. The dial on the wall was present here also. Lask pointed to an object attached to the wall, and it, too, was in the form of a tiny equilateral triangle. He pretended to push it and then acted out as if he would arrive in the room, indicating the button would summon him. He then showed me an alcove behind a sliding door that had what I assumed was a shower stall for washing. There was a triangular opening in the wall, low to the floor. I looked at my host who saw that I appeared puzzled, which he quickly tried to remedy. He walked to the opening and acted as if he was pulling up his gray robe and sitting in the niche. I nodded and smiled, realizing it was a toilet, and Lask grinned in return, appearing glad that I was no longer confused.

Lask took one of the books from a shelf, opened it, and handed it to me. Besides my love of science, I was always proficient in languages, having learned Latin, Italian, French, Spanish, and German. The reading material had the format of a vocabulary and grammar guide, complete with exercises and pictures associated with words. Lask then turned on the monitor. There were buttons on its base that controlled the volume and changed channels. There was an application which contained what appeared to be video games to choose from. There were also what we would consider to be reality shows, since a quick review of them showed the inhabitants in various locales performing tasks at the command of a host. Some of these activities included carrying heavy loads or balancing objects so they would not fall. There was one selection that viewed the populace in their real-time activities, similar to what the monitors in the first room showed. Lask then turned off the monitor and gestured to the bed, followed by him bending his head onto his clenched hands and closing his eyes. I nodded my head and was grateful to have some time to rest. Lask went to the entrance, pushed a button on the wall that dimmed the lighting, leaving me alone with my thoughts.

Chapter Six

I continued to use my micro-digital recorder to add to the entries in my log. I spent several months in Lask's home, learning the Burc language and other aspects of the lives of the natives by viewing day-to-day activities on the monitor in my room. Lask allowed me access to the main observation center in his home occasionally to observe several screens at once. I was frustrated that Lask did not let me explore the whole house, although he suggested with his arms by spreading them incrementally apart that he would grant me access to more of the dwelling later. He implied that I had to exercise patience by spreading his hands with the palms downward and moving them up and down, as if to convey that I should try to slow down my curiosity drive. While observing his gesturing I thought my host would be quite good at playing charades. Despite being excited to explore this different civilization, I still felt exasperated that I had substituted one prison on earth for another here.

I was able to go outside to enjoy a sectioned off parcel of land that was behind a tall, locked fence. Lask seemed to realize that I would need a break from my mental activities and provided me with a schematic and some rudimentary tools to build what looked like a picnic table. During those periods when I became weary of studying the language of the locals, I spent time outdoors constructing the table.

The planet was mostly cloudy, but at times the star that served as the planet's sun would appear. It seemed smaller than Earth's sun, either because it was indeed not as large, or perhaps more distant. In any event, it burned with enough intensity to adequately warm the planet. The amount of daylight was definitely shorter than the hours between the rising and setting of the sun on Earth, so darkness wrapped the planet for a longer period here, as if encouraging its occupants to sleep more.

While involved in my woodworking project, I thought of the times I spent with my father helping to make tables and cabinets. He loved working with his hands, and it was for him a sort of physical poetry as he put together various pieces of wood and formed them into a beautiful whole. For me, I not only enjoyed being with him, but the carpentry allowed me to focus on tasks that had completed outcomes.

When I finished my table project, I felt a sense of pride and hoped that I would dine outside with my host on it. However, I was shocked and enraged when one of the robots approached my completed work and smashed it with several powerful blows. I began to yell at the unfeeling chunk of machinery.

"You ugly pile of metal! How dare you touch what I made! You have no right!"

I just needed to vent my anger even though I knew the thing only responded to voice commands from those its programming permitted. It then removed the splintered remains and brought me more wood to start all over again. I continued to yell at the mechanical creature for a while. But then I realized the robot's action was consistent with how the way of life here kept the planet's populace constantly, although illogically, busy. Creation followed by dismantling and recreation was a cyclical behavior that turned back on itself instead of advancing forward. For a scientist like me, who yearned for progress, it was an infuriating practice.

I used my monitor to play the numerous video games as a source of diversion. Most of them were electronic versions of jigsaw puzzles. There were various levels of complexity, but I reached the top level of them quickly, so I did not feel they were particularly challenging. There was nothing in these games that pushed one to involved levels of analysis or theoretical hypothesizing.

I found the same rudimentary approach in the reading material once I began to decipher the language. From the workbooks present, I discovered that the name of the planet I was on translated in English to "Burc." The language of the Burcs was monosyllabic. It sounded guttural, almost like grunting. I discovered early on that if I was to communicate with Lask, I had to learn his language because he became frustrated and irritated beyond using some basic nouns and verbs I introduced to him in English. The Burc language seemed to be devoid of metaphors or similes. except when invoking what appeared to be historical references to ancient ancestors involving laws and rules. Also, for some inexplicable reason, these apparent founders of their civilization sometimes had longer names.

My observations while viewing life on the planet revealed that the Burcs lived a life of rigid routines. The clock alarms sounded nine times a day. They signaled when to sleep, to wake, to work, and to eat. No overlap from one set period into another occurred. Rarely did the high-pitched warning sound triggered by the implanted glowing forehead crystals ring out as they did when I first arrived. Sentries quickly removed from the sight of others those whose crystals did trigger the alerts. Burcs worked in groups that were color-coordinated. They ate at cubicles located in their segregated work areas, and socialization occurred in small time intervals within the same pigmented rooms. The break times consisted of workers participating in various puzzle games. They also engaged in group exercise programs, which consisted of numerous routines that involved running in circles, push-ups, sit-ups, and weight training. I also noted that individuals would perform exercises after work hours in their homes, once in the evening and three times on days off from work.

There were manuals about their jobs and pamphlets concerning rules of conduct. There was one of these pamphlets on my room's bookcase and I scanned its contents. It prescribed behavior down to the smallest details, including putting on the right foot work boot and right-hand glove before the placement of the boot and glove on the left appendages. There was also a requirement to go to the restroom six times a day.

I had hoped to experience this planet and its inhabitants and learn more about the history of the culture. But, I realized that the confining nature of this world would eventually shackle my intellectual curiosity, so I decided to look for a chance to escape when the opportunity presented itself.

While I was practicing my new language skills, a loud siren with a low base tone sounded, rattling the building and startling me to the point that I almost fell out of my chair. I had not heard this alarm before on Burc, and I wondered if its purpose was the same as the air raid test signals back on earth. Lask rushed into my room and indicated that I should stay where I was. His eyes looked tired, and I thought, sad. After he left, I put on the viewer console and chose the channel that monitored the inhabitants. There were few Burcs outside and I assumed many had retreated to their places of work or their homes. Terror began circulating through me and I rapidly gathered up my belongings as well as some clothing and food supplies in the backpack I had brought from the Seeker. I knew the way back to my spacecraft and could retrieve the HOPS transducer in case I had the opportunity to escape.

Another of the deep bass alerts sounded. I looked at the monitor and saw five spacecraft high above the community. I observed that each vessel was in the shape of a figure-eight. These ships began to swiftly disperse in an erratic pattern. The crafts emitted piercing white light aimed at the surface. Out of the ground, large shields appeared which rotated and shifted their opaque surfaces. Several intercepted the rays. They dissipated the beams into tiny streaks that then evaporated. However, when the shields were not quick enough to capture the attacking light blasts, the matter at the site of the hit turned to liquid and then to a gas before completely dispersing into the atmosphere. The beams evaporated several structures that housed Burcs. A deep vibrating sound emanated from the central, tall pyramid-shaped building that I noted upon my arrival. The sound became louder and then projected away from the planet's surface. When the sound encountered one of the alien craft, the spaceship stopped moving, as if caught in atmospheric quicksand. Its surface started to throb, and then, as if some large hands began to squeeze the craft, it imploded, accompanied by an explosion.

Three of the other ships suffered the same fate. However, the fifth was able to out-maneuver the sound blasts and attempted a suicide attack directly aiming itself at the central building. One of the sound blasts deflected it without destroying the spacecraft, and the alien ship hit a side of the building before crashing to the ground. On my monitor I saw Lask, who had found his way to the outside of the central Burc building. He then addressed the citizens with what I could make out were reassuring words that suggested that the attack was an opportunity for more work to rebuild what the enemy had destroyed.

When Lask eventually visited me, I asked, "Who are they?" so that I might learn about the alien attackers. I already discovered that this society did not encourage questioning, although the Burcs did tolerate inquisitiveness from the young who, as my father would say, "didn't know any better." However, I learned that if one posed a question, an individual should frame it to elicit an exact answer.

"They are Domandosemprians," Lask said. The length of the name produced a look on his face that sucking on a rancid lemon would elicit. "We have been at war with them for a long time." Lask made me understand that Burc historical documents noted that the confrontation started when some of the Domandosemprian ships landed on his planet. The visitors said they were explorers, but they quickly condemned Burc ways and said they wanted to "free" them. The aliens questioned everything and spent their lives debating and advancing more and more hypotheses and theories, and then testing them, but they never were satisfied with the results. For every situation they offered a banquet buffet of choices. The Burcs fought back, and the fight for the dominance of each planet's view on how to live escalated.

"There has been much death. Some of my race want this war to stop. In fact ..." He had his mouth open as if he was going to continue, but instead stopped short, as if he had said too much. "I must make plans to help those who are hurt."

"Will you not mourn the dead?" I asked.

"Too much thought of death makes one sad," said Lask. "Best not to dwell on it. I will see you soon."

As he left, I felt that probably too many deaths had weighed Lask down even more than the burdensome gravity of the planet.

Chapter Seven

As I grew more proficient in the Burc language, the conversations with Lask became more revealing. I found out that the size and configuration of the Seeker did not alert the planet's defenses as an immediate threat, since it differed from the Domandosemprian vessels. He also informed me that the topography made about half of the planet too precarious in which to live. He told me he held the title of "Proc," and he was one of the nine who occupied that office, one for each sector of the planet. There was a "Top Proc" who presided above the others. The job of the Procs was to be protectors of the people.

"What does the Proc shield them from?" I asked.

"From what is strange," said Lask. "A Proc can do things that most Burcs do not want to do to shield us. It is a curse that comes down through the years. My dad was a Proc, and so will my boy be one."

He said these words with his head bowed, and he ended with a sigh. He continued to provide information in a flat tone, almost as if what he spoke was memorized. I learned that the Procs were meant to insulate their people, not only from physical harm, but also from their own curiosity. His position at the top of the Burc hierarchy was not a revered one. The "curse" that Lask referred to was that a Proc's duty was a weighty and disturbing task of gathering and analyzing information, followed by deciding how to deal with it. He absorbed the anxiety over making decisions so his people would not have to endure psychological pain. That was why there were no "thought" crystals embedded in Lask's forehead. His job was "to free the Burcs from thoughts and the harm from them so the land was one and strong." But this work was so distasteful, other Burcs shunned him.

Lask said he was sorry that I must remain separate from the population, but it was necessary because it not only protected the inhabitants, it also kept me safe.

"You are strange," Lask said. "To us, you could be a threat."

I considered what Lask said about overthinking everything.

"My dad taught me to stick to set acts so as not to think too much," I said.

Lask nodded and said, "He must have felt that you had to curb your mind."

I thought how I longed to be a creature of habit to deal with my feverish mental inquisitions that threatened to consume me. So, I could understand, to a point, why the Burcs wanted to preserve their way of life. However, the part of me that wished to break free of set ways led me to pretend to be a superhero when I was young, someone who could fly in the sky and soar above earthly confines.

Lask said that his people would call me a "thore," the word for "outsider" on Burc. Most of the time beings in this area of space avoided Burc, knowing that the inhabitants did not welcome outside contact. When they did land on Burc, it was usually an emergency. Lask said he was performing his sacrificial role as Proc to deal with me to prevent any spread of my disturbing presence. Lask volunteered to deal with all thores. However, he confided to me that he secretly found interacting with alien life forms interesting.

Lask made up a story for the community that stated I was possibly a creature from a place known as Syntharm. There were rumors of the existence of such a world, but they were mostly part of mythological lore. The proportions of the size of my head to my body did correspond to accounts of what a Syntharmian's appearance would look like. Lask told the other Procs that I had made contact with the Domandosemprians as a diplomatic gesture. But, I used one of their ship's escape pods to land on Burc to avoid the intense interrogation of those in charge on the planet. He had quarantined the pod to avoid encounters that would provoke curiosity. Lask's official statement was that he was attempting to communicate with me to learn of enemy plans. It would appear like his task to keep me in his hut for a long time made sense. However, I did not really know how he felt about me, and what his intentions were regarding my presence there.

Following a period of roughly six Earth months when I continued to study the language and observe the Burcs, Lask finally asked me about the Seeker's capabilities. I was reluctant to tell him. He assured me that he would program the robots not to divulge its existence, and in fact, Lask said he wanted to make sure others would not discover it. He noted that the usual practice with a new find was to ensure an otherworldly object was not an imminent threat by having a Proc analyze it. If it was not useful for defensive or enforcement purposes, it was destroyed to eliminate harmful speculations over something novel which might lead to anxiety and disruption among the populace.

"How do I know you will not take it if I tell you where it is?" I asked him.

He chuckled before answering.

"If I wished to have your ship I could have found it by now. I want you to keep your craft in case you need to go if I can't shield you, or the war gets worse."

I decided to trust Lask, but I did not tell him about the hidden transducer. Frank also had devised an elaborate encryption sequence of numbers and letters that only I knew would activate the device. Lask had questions about the Seeker's ability to travel over large areas of space. I showed him by extrapolating on star maps in the study approximately where I came from. Lask realized it was an immense distance I had traveled and immediately asked about the propulsion system. I gave him a quick outline of the conversion process and its hazards. He looked worried and said that the technology of the HOPS transformation into high density or infinite matter would make it a formidable weapon. As I listened to Lask's alarmed voice, I knew he was no Rutlaw. He wanted to prevent deaths and end the war with the Domandosemprians. I told him where the Seeker was, and he promised to keep its existence a secret and use the robots (which in Burc would be equivalent to our word "bots") to keep it hidden.

I eventually convinced Lask that I had to get out among the people not only because I was feeling claustrophobic, but also to find out more about the Burcs. Lask was resistant at first, concerned about the negative consequences of my wandering beyond his residence. However, he eventually agreed to a short field trip. To compensate for the strong gravitational force, over time the inhabitants had developed increased muscle girth. I felt squashed down, especially when I had to ascend any heights. Luckily there were few elevated areas.

Tunts was the name of the city that was not far from where I landed. The dense air mixture produced an oppressive feeling, and I was alarmed that its denseness might choke me on prolonged exertion. There was an oxygen supply unit built into the clothing of the locals and many Burcs wore air masks to compensate for the poor breathing conditions. I saw that there were several factories about, belching smoke into the air through stacks, which contributed to the breathing problem. The robes I wore along with my air mask disguised my appearance, ensuring that I would not set off any crystal alerts.

Walking for long distances emphasized the pull of the planet's gravity on my unaccustomed body. Lask pointed to the swampy areas I noticed when I first landed. He said that there was a drainage problem on the planet, and communities sometimes sank and disappeared. Despite the problem, there were parcels of land which contained buildings which, except for the central pyramidal one, were long and low, and fashioned into triangular shapes. There were no skyscrapers trying to scale the heavens. The industrial buildings consisted of heavy materials, such as brick and stone. I asked Lask about using alternative lightweight substances, but he said this manner of construction was the way for them over the years. There were also residential sections where workers and their families lived. Fences separated each piece of land from the others, and each section housed the same worker occupation. Even in the center of the city, the buildings had walls and fences enclosing the edifices. Indeed, a stone wall surrounded the whole of Tunts, with openings at various places to exit and enter. Bots guarded those spots.

"I have tried to seek new ways. But, what has been, is strong with us," said Lask. "Most feel it to be bad to change what is. What is new leads to more thoughts, more why's and how's, that cause more of the same. It is thought when Burcs think, all else stops. Most say we can't both think and do at the same time."

Attached to a metal obelisk in the center square of the city was a larger version of the rotating equilateral triangular dial that was in my room in Lask's residence. As Lask and I passed by the object, it sounded one of its high-pitched alerts which I recognized signaled the start of a feeding period. Local citizens brought food out from the surrounding buildings and everyone sat at three-pointed tables. We had juice and bread for breakfast not long ago. Yet, Lask began to eat the fowl and root vegetable meal that was often prepared on Burc. Despite the long walk, I was not ready for something so soon after breakfast. Lask surveyed the Burcs looking our way. Lask said to me, "You must eat at the right time."

"I can't eat so much food," I said. "I see why there is such a brief time from one meal to the next. The pull of the land's force is strong; thus, you need more food as fuel. But I, as of yet, am not used to ..."

"Do not speak more," said Lask in a whisper. "Such talk must not be heard. The times to eat and drink are part of The Code of old. Our way is not to think, but to act. You must learn the ways of the Burcs while you are here."

On our city journey I saw bakeries, food stores, and clothing establishments, along with carpenters and masons performing their jobs. There were many types of professions that employed tools similar to those used in nineteenth century America. The camera equipment connected to the observational screens, the robotic enforcement squad, and defense mechanisms were quite advanced. However, technology did not replace time-consuming labor. It seemed as if everyone I saw was working, keeping busy. If one completed a task ahead of schedule, such as making clothing, the Burc then removed the stitches and the sewing process began again, just like other illogical work cycles I witnessed.

We then arrived at the tall, wide-based building that tapered to a point in the sky that stood in the middle of this Burc zone. Lask ushered me inside the first-floor chamber, saying, "This is where we keep The Code." The large room, like the edifice that contained it, had a vast triangular-shaped floor and walls that slanted to a peaked ceiling. Windows had paintings that depicted battles where Burcs appeared tall with weapons in their hands, mostly spears and swords, as they stood over vanquished creatures that were on the ground. The defeated enemies were small compared to their conquerors, and their distinguishing feature was that they had large heads.

There were many Burcs there silently moving down a central gray aisle made of stone away from the entrance toward a raised section at the other end of the hall. They stopped to kneel in front of a gold-framed, glass covered document. Lask led me to the encased scripture, which had a sign above it that read "The Code of Laws." While Lask bowed his head in silence for a while, I noticed that there were other smaller protected documents on either side of the centerpiece. Outside I asked Lask what they were. He said that they contained the story of how the Gens, the Burc ancestors, overcame the enemies of the state. They also detailed the generations of the names of the Gens.

"But, the list is not whole, and does not state the names of the first Gens," Lask said. "We are not sure why, but we are told not to ask," he said, shrugging his shoulders as if unsure of the edict.

Back at Lask's house (the better translation would be "hut"), Lask explained that whenever "thores" came, they did not stay at a Proc's hut. There were buffer-like places below the surface to house them. Bots would deal with the thores, including conducting interrogations. But, Lask wanted to know more about where I came from, and thus fabricated the security reasons for my staying at his hut. Lask prohibited me from meeting his family to avoid shock and resulting disturbance. I could, however, observe their actions through my viewer to get to know them, which turned out to be for the better, and for the worse.

Chapter Eight

My now excellent Burc language skills allowed me to have more informative meetings with Lask. The early discussions consisted mostly of me asking questions. Lask answered briefly and reluctantly, which showed he was not used to interrogation. He did not ask many questions about my personal life or my world at this point.

I accessed recordings of retaliations against the Domandosemprians. Burc bots manned star ships that attacked the home planet of the enemy with their imploding weapons and destroyed inhabited areas. Lask said he argued against targeting the civilian population unless necessary, but many times the majority of the Procs voted him down.

The largest Burc industry was the manufacturing of clothing. There were wardrobes for various occasions. There was a variety of cloaks, hats, shoes, buckles and belts produced. From what I saw, an individual's apparel conveyed a place in the society. For example, a laborer wore deep brown fabric and a black metal belt, as well as a black hat and cape when dining out. Foremen donned blue overalls and hoods at work, and blue tunics and gloves when doing chores at home. Lask did not wear the layers that the others wore, and instead always donned a version of the light gray robe I first saw him wearing. It seemed to me that the darker the clothing and the more layers worn garnered a higher regard in this society, which meant that manual laborers received bows and pleasantries as they walked in public areas.

Another observation I recorded was that there were sayings in huge letters on billboards and on walls. The two I saw most often, as best as I could translate, were, "Stick to The Code," and "More work, less thought." I eventually asked Lask to provide more information about "The Code."

"That is a hard thing to tell," he said, and he paused with his lips pressed together. I could see that he struggled with providing long explanations. But, I knew he wanted to educate me about his planet, for what reason I did not yet realize.

"The Code is the tale of our race, and guides us how to live," he said, looking upward, as if in reverence. "The Gens ("Founders," I eventually determined would be the best word to describe them) gave it to us at the time of the Great Quake (not a natural upheaval, but a social one, I learned). The Gens, before they were gone, saved us from the Great Quake, and the facts of it. We long to know of the past they hid since it is the tale of who we are. But The Code says not to ask."

Lask paused, and his eyes shifted to me and then away, as if making sure no one was around. He cringed a bit, as if he was about to say something upsetting.

"There is a myth," he said, "that the Gens before the Great Quake still live, and that they will come back in some form so we can be saved once more. It is a hope as we fear a new Quake may soon come."

There were lines of worry on Lask's forehead as he uttered those words. He continued, saying, "The Domandosemprians hurt us more and more. They have no fear. They seem not to care about death. And, the Top Proc is ill, and what makes that worse is he is the last of his line."

From my observations of Burc culture, I understood the gravity of the situation. The cornerstone of the Burc civilization was based upon familial hierarchy and interrelationships. The head of each family unit could be either female or male, the leadership depending upon the tradition in each family unit. The spouse was in charge when the mate died or was no longer able to lead the family. Burcs worshipped the connection that bound relatives together. There existed a rigid segregated class structure that rested upon the work that the individuals performed. But, despite this vocational separation, the adoration for family cemented the Burcs together. It even seemed that they felt that all Burcs were related. The physical harming, let alone killing, of another Burc was a punishable offense.

I already learned that the male's place in the society determined that of the eldest son, and the mother's position designated that of her first-born daughter. If the male was the family head and he had only daughters, then the eldest female would be the chief authority in that unit once the male passed away. There was no room for fluctuations due to chance or personal preference. With no offspring to take the Top Proc's place while under increased attack from the enemy, the stress of instability would threaten the Burc foundation of society.

"The lack of an heir must have come up in the past, yes?" I asked Lask.

"Yes," he said, "but all of those in the Top Proc's line have died. He is the lone one of his tribe. In the past there has been at least one. It is the first in known times there is no sure claim. I fear the Procs will fight to see who will lead. There is no good to come of this right now while the war costs so much."

I looked at Lask and he saw my arched eyebrows and shrugged shoulders, which suggested that he had to try something new to help his people.

"I know," he said. "I have learned from you that there are more ways to live. But we are not good with change. Our rules have worked for us for a long time. We need to end the war so we can heal. But, The Code says to not let the Domandosemprians win."

Lask shook his head.

"The road on which we must go will be a hard one," he said.

Chapter Nine

Despite being far from home, on an alien world, I was more curious than afraid. I set out to explore, and the scientist part of me was excited to discover what for me was a new frontier. I would not experience any form of satisfaction until I had closer contact with the Burcs. I thought that the easiest way to gain access was through Lask's family. He had told me his wife, Lure, died. He became tearful just stating the fact of her passing five Burc years prior. He said she was wise and he had consulted with her about any problems that arose. Lask said she was also a caring mother who protected her children from harmful thoughts.

He had two children, a boy and a girl. I had seen them on the viewer. The daughter's name was Og. I guessed she was close to thirteen years of age by Earth standards. She was thin with a somewhat pointy face, as if she wanted to poke into spaces to discover what was within. The boy was closer to the age of twenty in Earth years and his name was Pots. He was muscular and had squinty eyes. When I suggested that I meet the youths, Lask was not enthusiastic. He said I would disrupt their lives, but I already heard from him that they wondered about a secret person in their home.

"You are a thore," Lask said, but he didn't have to remind me that I was an outsider. "They have been taught in school that you are like a germ that can spread and harm."

"You have said that your boy and girl ask of me," I countered. "Is it not a good thing to let them know, and put an end to these thoughts?"

Lask looked at me with unblinking eyes before speaking again.

"I knew this would be. I had hoped it would not. From what you have told me, your kind shows some Domandosemprian ways. But your words are sound. It shall be done."

I learned that Burcs can have up to three children, but after the third, the mother underwent sterilization. The population control was an attempt to protect against the overconsumption of resources. Lask told his children that they must be ready to make the sacrifice of a Proc family, and deal with a thore. When he brought in Og and Pots, I thought that their thought crystals would sound the alarm once they met me. But because Pots would be a future Proc, he had no alarms implanted in his forehead. Og did, but Lask held a short wand in his hand that I assumed jammed any signal coming from her crystals. The son and daughter seemed afraid and anxious, and held each other's hands with their fingers interlaced, as if forming a chain link fence to protect them from the questions that were springing into their minds. Pots began to speak in a halting manner.

"If one lives on Burc," he said, "one must eat, sleep, and work. The thore, Sam, lives on Burc, so he eats, sleeps, and works here like us."

Og continued her brother's thoughts.

"To live in Lask's hut, one must do chores. You live in Lask's hut, so, Sam, you must do chores."

Og then went out of the room and shortly returned with towels, a bucket of hot water and bottles of liquid. Og then showed me how I should mix the ingredients, and then the two of them left so I could clean my room. They had, at least initially, fit me into their world, and for now that was enough. I was there to work. I thought that if I had met an alien from another world on Earth, I would have a million questions, and I would need a long time to ponder the answers later. But here, on Burc, they turned an enigma into a janitor.

"For now, that is all they can do," said Lask, and he smiled and left.

***

The gender of the head of the household determined the duties in the family on Burc. Lask had said there were female heads in other houses, and some Procs were women. Since in Lask's home, the male was the head. Thus, Og, the only female relative, did the domestic chores, which included handling finances, hiring contractors, and performing maintenance of the house's systems. She was also studying to be a teacher to assist other households with children in learning the ways of the Burcs. Apparently because I was a thore, it was excusable for me as a male in the house to do the female's designated work. But, I had to complete the activities according to Og's routine, which was the way of the Burcs.

Unlike our planet, I learned that there were twenty-seven hours in a day, nine days in a week, six weeks in a month, and eighteen months in a year on Burc. The number three and its multiples were used often, I assumed, because that's how many sides there were in a triangle, and their society was hierarchical. Also, the worship of the geometric shape mirrored the shape of the Burcs themselves, since their heads were small in proportion to their bodies.

Burcs cleaned the waste-room, or toilet area, first, during the ninth slot of the first workday, about nine o'clock on a Monday, in Earth terms. The clean-room, or bathroom, which was close to the waste-room, was next on the list. Then came the rest-rooms, or bedrooms, and the remainder of the up-hut, or second floor of the building. Then we attacked the down-hut, which included the cook-space, eat-place, and the clothes-room, where we did the laundry. I imagined that washing clothes would be quite a task among the laborers on Burc, due to the numerous layers of clothing.

The layout of the hut was like the one in the house where my family lived. The Burcs had to clean each area within certain time periods, and if one room wasn't finished before the next was to be cleaned, then the prior space was left half-done. There was no deviation allowed in the step-by-step process. In the cook-space, I had to wash the eating utensils first, then came the bowls, and then the cups. I said to Og that I didn't see the reason why everything had to be done in that order. She shook her head and smiled as if she was dealing with an ignorant child and then said The Code stated, "One step out of place, the whole hut falls on your face."

The living area of the hut was made of several types of stones. There were slate floors, stucco-like walls, and marble-appearing counters. They even fashioned the closets out of some sort of petrified substance. Since I was not familiar with the hut early on, I would make a wrong turn occasionally and would receive some bruises when I bumped into a rigid living space angle.

One day men came with tools and a cart full of slate planks. They proceeded to take apart the roof of the house, and replace it with a new one. I had not noticed any rain getting in or ceiling damage. I asked Og why the men were there.

"They are roof men," she said. "There is a roof to be made. They do their job."

"But your roof is fine," I said.

Og seemed rattled by my statement, moving her head from side to side, as if searching for a response.

"We make new roofs in six years. It has been six years since the last new roof. So, it is time for a new roof on our hut," Og argued syllogistically.

"But you don't need one," I persisted.

Her eyes darted about, looking like she wanted to find an escape route. But she also wanted to convince me or possibly even herself of her argument.

"I said the same to Pots. But, he said they need to do their jobs. He quoted The Code: 'The more you work at it, the less you think of it,' it says." And with that, Og went off to do gardening, planting root vegetables along with what looked like squash and peppers. Everything there was edible. There were no flowers visible, which would have added a non-practical aesthetic element to the area.

***

I recorded a conversation I had with Pots to include in my log. He was to be married within the year. I asked a direct question about the romantic process on Burc.

"How did you meet the one you will wed?"

Pots said, "The boy and girl of two Procs join. I am such a boy, and such is what I will do. Our groups matched me and my mate at age three. It is our way."

"Yes, but what do you feel for her?" I asked.

I knew that Lask told his children that it was fine to discover things about me, but that would entail enduring my distasteful questions. Pots pondered what I said.

"I felt good that I did not have to care how to find a mate," he said.

"But are there no steps that have to do with love?" I asked.

Pots zeroed in on the "steps" part of my question since that seemed to focus him on where he felt most comfortable. He told me there was a social ritual which involved youths going out on group dates with other young people in addition to their matches. All liaisons were platonic, and the young people stayed within social group boundaries. Pots said that one became part of a larger Burc community this way. Males and females formed brotherhoods and sisterhoods, so that all felt part of a group family. There was adult supervision to ensure no breach of proper sexual conduct. Burcs did not allow sex prior to the joining of a couple since it could lead to chaotic wonderings about who to be with, which led to jealousies and hurt feelings. But, within a joined relationship, the community encouraged sex. They considered physical intimacy an experience that blocked out unneeded thoughts. The Burcs found marital sex satisfied basic needs and, thus, they admired it. Plus, it made babies which occupied the parents with tasks to care for the offspring. Also, sex added to the population, within the prescribed limitations, so there would be more workers and soldiers who could help with the fight against the Domandosemprians.

***

The Burc way of life made me think about my mother who had her own routine that followed a cleaning cycle. Even though her passion was science, being a high school physics teacher, she felt satisfaction after doing her house chores. My father relied on his military training to keep him grounded. Yet he felt one with the sea when he sailed. He let go of all his regulated side when he was on that infinite expanse of flowing water. They seemed to find a balance in life. I looked to them as models. But my mother died of brain cancer in her early thirties. I endured mental suffering from watching her insightful mind diminish into nothingness. My father's death in the Turkish War left me devastated and I could not find the harmony that my parents felt in life. Arthur felt the pain of those losses but somehow found relief from his books and writing, tools that didn't work for me.

My thoughts led me to ask Og about Burc religious beliefs, wondering if they found solace in areas of faith. She said that even though her people ate meat and consumed fruits and vegetables, they worshiped animals and vegetation for their simple nature. They especially revered non-thinking inorganic substances, such as rocks, soil, fire, and water. There were weekly gatherings at temples where the Burcs attended to show how much they envied the purity of the parts of their world that existed with single purposes and had no need for questions. Sometimes, when a Burc finished work or play and felt too many thoughts starting to invade one's brain, he or she would do a form of meditation. The individual would lie still and pretend to be an object, such as a brick wall, and would repeat, "I am a brick wall. I am a brick wall," until the Burc believed that he or she was one and the same with that thing.

I observed a religious meeting on the viewer. The stone building where many Burcs gathered had seats made of rock. There was a celebrant, called an Ellc, who stood on a raised stage wearing several layers of vestments whose colors were black and white. He held a sparkling crystal in one hand and a chunk of tree bark in the other. He raised them up above his head and said, "Praise those things which have no thought, and those Burcs that wish to be like them. For they shall have no pain of the mind." The Ellc then began to juggle the bark and crystal. He then spun around three times, and moved three steps to the right and then three steps to the left. He finished by kneeling and standing up three times. He then moved to the side and each member of the congregation brought his or her own objects, including fruits and root plants, to the center of the stage in succession, and repeated the same actions. The practice was quite time-consuming.

After those present finished participating, the Ellc gave a sermon.

"I am me, and you are thee, and all of us are we," he began. "They who wrote The Code, bless them. (He bowed and the others did the same). They sought to make us free. Free from too much choice; free from too much to want; free from too much time to think of things that make us hurt. We work the jobs the cursed Procs give us; we play the games the Procs made for us; we watch their shows; we eat; we dance the old way and sing the old songs; we make love with our mates. It is all we need."

After what I heard from Og and seeing the religious ceremony, I felt the allure of not having to worry about all the decisions to think about back on Earth. One had to ruminate about what to study in college, what job to prepare for, and how to pay the bills and stay healthy. One wondered who to date, and how to act with that person. There had to be decisions as to who were the best people to lead the countries. We questioned how to fix laws if they were inadequate. Wouldn't it be nice to be a tree, firmly rooted, raising its branches to the sun, drinking the moisture from the ground, and feeling the breezes blow through the leaves? I practiced the Burc meditation and pretended to be that tree. It was nice, for a while. But then, my mind began to wander. I thought about how the Burcs and Domandosemprians came to be. How did the fighting start? Who wrote The Code? How can the Burcs be happy without exploration and discovery? And on and on, until I no longer felt like a tree.

Chapter Ten

One day when Og and I were alone outside doing some gardening, she came closer to me. Her bushy, reddish-brown hair hung in front of her face, almost shielding her mouth. She looked around first and pulled out the wand that Lask used to block her crystals from going off. I immediately realized she was revealing to me her rebellious act of turning off the alarm, so for protection I motioned that we should move closer to the house wall to avoid the surveillance cameras mounted on the roof. After we reached the unobserved spot, I asked why she had the wand. Og looked downward and whispered that she had overheard discussions between her father and other Procs about forbidden topics the rest of the Burcs should not discuss. Instead of repelling her, what she heard drew her curiosity. She said that she would use the wand and covertly access her father's books and screens when Lask was away and her brother was otherwise occupied. She did not have many opportunities to learn much, but what she did discover intrigued her. She said their schools taught basic skills and provided information specific to each person's assigned duties.

"I have thoughts," she said to me, shaking like a guilty sinner in a confessional booth. "I think what it would be like to go to where the stars are. Get to know far off worlds. To find how things live there. How does it all work and fit for them."

I was surprised by her curiosity, and I did not know how to proceed. I knew my presence already posed a problem. I did not want to interfere, but I also felt that staying silent might foster wrong assumptions. Also, I very much felt drawn to the possibility of having a meaningful discussion with another explorer since this world fostered a rigid stay-in-your-place ethic. But, I worried about what would happen to her if others discovered her inquiries. I put my finger to my lips to signal the need for quiet. She looked sad at my refusal to discuss her dilemma as I walked back to the rows of earth ready to receive their seeds. But in the days that followed, Og persisted in getting us alone and asking about Syntharmian females. I found a hidden outside spot and decided to respond to some of her questions.

"First, I am not a Syntharmian. I don't know what a Syntharmian is. I am from Earth, a world far from here," I said. "What is it you want to know?"

Og's eyes widened and she began to ask if those on Earth studied about such things as animals, the weather, and the stars. I explained how boys and girls also went to schools where I came from. I told her as they grew older they studied the sciences of geology, chemistry, biology, and physics, and explained what those disciplines explored. I told her how scientists did experiments, collected data to understand existence, and invented things, hopefully, to make life better. It was difficult for me to translate complicated terms, so I used the Burc words for "rocks," "how things join," "things that live," and "forces."

"I like to draw what I see, and write tales," she said. "Do you have that on your Earth?"

I told her that we studied the arts, and that people painted, sculpted, wrote stories, and made videos so they could express their thoughts.

"So, those like you go to far off worlds?" she asked.

I told her we did but only to a few moons and planets close by. But this response did not satisfy her.

"If that is so, how did you come here?" she asked.

Now I knew our conversation could lead to trouble.

"I made a ship," I said. "It can travel far. I came here with it."

Og jumped up and down, smiling, and pushed her small face with her pointy nose right next to mine. She wanted to know how my spacecraft worked, and would I be using it to visit other planets. I illustrated on her own drawing paper to give her a basic overview of what I had invented. She clapped her hands as if to applaud what I achieved.

"Life here is so dull," she said. "I think of what the point of it all is, to do the same each day. To see new sights, to learn new things, thrills me. I know I am not meant to think this way. If found out, it could be bad."

I tried to reassure her that I would say nothing about her questions, and that she could trust me. She was grateful for my promise.

We had many secret meetings following that first one. She started by just wanting to know about practical matters, how people on Earth cooked, cleaned, and worked. But then she was interested in how the society functioned financially and logistically. She was surprised at the freedom individuals had to choose what to study and do with their lives. She was particularly amazed at how some pursued investigations as to the meaning of existence, and explored matters of faith that extended beyond nature in the form of religious beliefs, which many times led to raising questions more than providing answers. When we touched on the topic of romance, she thought I was being untruthful when I said that people choose their own mates based on feelings of love. After a while, she said she felt dizzy, as if becoming overwhelmed with the possibilities.

"I have been matched with the son of a Proc," she whispered. She scrunched her face as if tasting something bitter. "I do not like him. He does not like to talk, and I do. When I speak, he shuts me up. There is a boy in my school who likes to speak of how to make our lives more fun. I want to be matched with him. He must watch out, though. If he wants to speak too much, he may get the Cure."

I wanted to comment about how most people on Earth would consider a young teenager not to be old enough to marry. I especially wished to find out what that "Cure" consisted of. But Og realized we must stop talking since we had been out of the observation area for an extended period. So, we resumed our labor.

I decided to ask Lask myself about the "Cure" Og mentioned. He was reluctant to tell me, apparently disturbed by the topic, and changed the subject when I brought it up. I decided that it was important to find out about the Cure, which meant I had to venture out on my own. I decided to wear my Burc disguise and sneak away one day. After learning about the technology of the bots, I realized that they went to charging stations where they entered a "sleep" mode to regenerate. I monitored the time of day when this activity occurred. Over time I noted all the blind spots in the surveillance system. One day when Lask was not at home, Og was at school, and Pots was preparing for his marriage, I exited the grounds while the bots were recharging.

During my previous outing, I had noticed a spot that contained a label that read "laij," which I later learned referred to a sort of detention facility. I went to the building and waited outside where many Burcs gathered. Eventually, two bots came out dragging three individuals who appeared sedated. They loaded these Burcs into an enclosed motorized tram, which differed from the open-air rudimentary transportation vehicle pulled by animals that farmers on Burc used. I followed the crowd of Burcs who accompanied the vehicle to a facility with a courtyard not far away. There were many more Burcs entering the area there. The bots took the drugged Burcs out of the vehicle, two males and one female, and placed them on a platform in full view of the citizens. They were secured in chairs in front of short poles that had metallic bullet-shaped hoods placed at their upper ends. A voice came over loudspeakers attached to the courtyard's jagged gray stone buildings.

"You are here to see these Burcs get the Cure. They broke the thought rules, as they felt the old ways must lead to new ones, which we know can bring us harm. For the good of us all, we must fix them," said the voice from the sky. The bots placed the cones over the heads of the bound Burcs. An increasingly deeper bass sound shook the stage, and most in the crowd winced. After about a minute, the sound decreased in volume and then eventually ceased after about five minutes. The bots removed the coverings. The speaker then asked simple questions of the Burcs on the stage.

"Do you know who you are?"

"Do you know what to do?

"Do you know how to be?"

The answer from all three captives to the questions was, "No."

"Good," said the Voice. "You three will now learn once more. Go forth, and live by The Code."

I had witnessed a type of lobotomy as a punishment for too much questioning. The bots then took the three Burcs inside the facility. Those in the courtyard disbanded, heading back to pursue their limited lives. I was shaking and felt sick to my stomach at seeing the wiping away of what little individuality these inhabitants had left. Yet, those around me showed no emotion, and said little except what chores they still had to complete. It was as if the gathering for what to me was a traumatic event was just another item for them on the day's agenda. I could see why Lask did not want to speak of the procedure I witnessed, since he was already doubting some of his society's ways. Yet, I felt that I must discuss with him what I had seen and attempt to discover what plans he had for his planet, and for me.

Chapter Eleven

There were other Domandosemprian attacks. The curved foreign crafts appeared and rained their light-producing, mass-to-gas transforming weapons down on the Burc's population. Most of the time the shielding worked, but not always, as before, and they caused the loss of lives and property. Because Lask's hut was at a substantial distance from the center of the local community, it and his family were lucky to escape any direct hits. When the alarms went off, the members of the household would go into underground shelters that felt claustrophobic to me, but which Lask and his children did not seem to mind. However, I observed an eroding of Lask's mental state. He looked exhausted and worried after meeting with other Procs, directing repairs due to the impact of the assaults, and reluctantly planning retaliatory raids against the enemy. But perhaps his conversations with me also shook the foundations of his besieged world. I optimistically talked about how populations of a few countries on Earth explored various points of view, compromised, and came to a consensus about how to govern which allowed individuals to pursue their happiness. I knew, however, that the relaxing of rigidity of viewpoints was disturbingly alien to the Burc way of life.

***

I felt I needed to keep my body in shape given the precarious situation I would be in if Lask's protection disappeared and I needed to defend myself or escape quickly. I worked out every day, placing myself on a kind of boot camp schedule, which was especially demanding given the increased gravity. Since the Burcs believed in the emphasis on the body, there was an exercise area in Lask's hut. I jogged on a track that circled the room, and used a bodybuilding bench that had triangular weights, with a bot spotting me. There was a rope that I used to climb to the top of the low peaked vaulted ceiling. The physical exertion often freed me from thoughts about the Burc civilization, and the possible threats to my life there. However, my curiosity about this world would interrupt my bodily calm occasionally as I exercised. I admitted to Lask that I witnessed the Cure. He nodded his head and sighed. I think he felt relief that he did not have to tell me about this traumatic practice, and I believe he definitely did not want to show it to me. One day, shortly following a Domandosemprian raid, Lask came to me and provided me with some answers to my questions.

"I have something to show you," he said.

He led me to a tram and a bot drove the two of us far out into an area beyond the city limits. We had to leave the tram to traverse a rocky area which was only accessible on foot. Lask carried a lantern with him. There were warning signs that prohibited approaching the area, and bots situated near our destination stood guard to prevent access to the spot. As we approached, Lask took out another of his wands and pressed a button on it. The bots went into sleep mode. Lask guided me down an embankment that had stairs made of stone to make it easier to descend. We traveled downward for a couple of hundred feet. When we reached the bottom, there was a flat landing and in front of us was an arched entrance to a cave that had carvings on it. They seemed to consist of a greeting in the Burc language, but it appeared to be in another dialect so I could not translate what was written there adequately. I looked to Lask for an explanation by raising eyebrows and shrugging my shoulders.

"This is what the Procs call The Safe," he said. "Our tribe found it years in the past, when we sought firm land on which to build. It looks like it has stood since the dawn of our time."

We walked closer to the entrance. I looked at the carved writing on the frame of the entrance. I drew closer and squinted, then clenched my mouth, which communicated my frustration to Lask.

"It is Burc, but some of the letters are not quite what we now use. We think the Gens made these marks. It is strange since some words are long," said Lask.

He walked up and pointed to a line of writing.

"This seems to say that we should go in," he said.

We walked through the arched opening into a dark room. Lask raised his lantern and spoke.

"The Gens gave us The Code of rules so that we could live to be free of too much thought. They gave us the tech to be used only to stop those who would take us to a lost place of the mind. The Code says to go to war with those who say to do what is not in The Code. But there are no words of war here."

Lask walked to the end of the chamber and the lantern showed an iron door with no handle or lock. He pointed to words carved above it.

"In fact," Lask said. "here it seems to say that the way to joy is through peace that comes when one joins with the foe. It also says to come in and learn of the past."

"Some, where I come from, feel one must find love for those foes, so all can work as one group," I said. "We also try to look at the faults of the past so as to do the right thing in the time that is to come."

"That seems wise," said Lask. "Has your race learned from what went before?"

I sighed. "Not so much when it comes to war," I said.

Lask went on to say that when the elder Procs discovered The Safe they were torn by the mixed messages that The Code and The Safe sent. Were they to fight or seek a truce with those that opposed what The Code preached? There were debates, which of course only Procs had permission in which to engage (but which they still found loathsome), as to whether to accept the invitation to enter The Safe. The Burcs revered their history that joined them together as a family. However, The Code instructed them not to be inquisitive beyond what they needed to simply survive.

In the end, the Proc Group decided to send one of their own into The Safe. Lask pointed to a button on the right-hand side of the portal, which he said when pushed slides the door open. However, the door closes once individuals enter and will not open until the visitors leave. After a few days, the Proc that the Council sent came back through the same door. He had no recollection of anything he saw or experienced inside The Safe, or anything that occurred in his life for the prior year. Lask said what the Proc endured was something like the memory wipe that the Burcs now use, and which they believed the Gens handed down to "cure" the overly curious. The ancient Procs were divided as to what to conclude. Some believed that The Safe was some sort of test that punished those that asked too many questions. Others suggested that one had to prove one's worth to learn the rest of the history of the Gens, and thus, the story of Burc. They decided to protect the site from detection and guard it. Over many years, some Procs ventured inside, only to have the memories of their experiences for the prior year expunged.

It was a dilemma, and being the inquisitive scientist that I am, I wanted to solve their problem. I was intrigued by what The Safe could reveal. My initial response was to side with those that believed the dwelling was a chance to discover the secrets of the Burc past, and possibly help them understand their evolution. I felt compelled to further aid their growth, since there was the possibility here to end a long war. I also had to admit to myself that my own battle against armed conflict added a personal element to my motivation to want to move the Burcs toward peace and an enlightened state of being through knowledge.

Before we left the chamber, I noticed that above the door was a figure etched into the wall. It looked like a capital "U" seated on a straight line that widened at the bottom into a triangle. I had not seen this illustration anywhere else on Burc. I asked Lask if he knew its meaning, but he said there was no knowledge of its significance. After we were outside again I expressed my thanks to Lask for giving me this information. But I could see that there was more he had to say.

"As I told you, there are some, like me, who want this war to cease," said Lask. "The Safe does not urge us to wage war. The words you saw say peace is the way to joy. I know you wish to learn why I have kept you from harm. There is a point."

He stopped for a moment, and I could sense that the increased gravity of the planet was not all that was weighing Lask down.

"I have a task for you. I want you to use your ship to go to Domandosempria. Your craft will not draw fire, as will a Burc one would. They will give in to their ways, and will want to ask who you are and where you came from. If you can say how you have been here and saw there are those of us who want to end the war, there might be a chance to gain that joy that peace can bring."

Chapter Twelve

I struggled with sleep that night after hearing Lask's request. My tossing one way and then the other reflected my conflicted feelings. I knew all too well about the devastation of war and if I could in any way help to end its deadly impact here, I hoped to have a sense of redemption for the role that I played in one of Earth's conflicts. But, I was a huge *Star Trek* fan, and could not stop thinking about the "Prime Directive," which stressed in that franchise's stories the importance of not interfering in the development of other alien cultures. Of course, my presence on the planet had already created a limited impact on Burc. However, what would happen if I became involved in an interplanetary dispute? My actions could affect the development of these two species. What right did I have to meddle in the affairs of other races? On the other hand, I could not escape the fact that these two worlds had been battling for such a long time with no end in sight, and the evolutionary progression seemed to have stagnated. What if I could work as a catalyst, an outside element that would facilitate the process of healing, but then extract myself without becoming the primary agent of change in the process?

Events did not allow me the luxury of time to think my way out of my dilemma. It was after I finally fell asleep a couple of hours before dawn when two bots entered my room and grabbed me. Lask entered behind them, and there was no smile on his face.

"Things have been found out," said Lask. "I am sad to say that the Procs think you are a risk to our way of life. They want to see you. I will be there and help if I can."

The bots whisked me into the back of a windowless tram. Lask could not accompany me. He said I would see him again at the Proc Group. I felt like I couldn't breathe inside the confining vehicle, as my lungs gasped for air and my mind grappled to understand what was happening. What caused the Procs to see me as a threat? Had they discovered Lask's plan to use me to contact the Domandosemprians? Did they find the Seeker? I decided that if that was the case, I would do whatever I had to, as I did on Earth, to prevent the Burcs from using my invention to further their war efforts.

The tram stopped and the bots pulled me from the vehicle. We had arrived at the tall pyramidal building, which I learned translated to the word "Hub," and which was the central governing point of this area of Burc. The bots escorted me through the lower level of the edifice where there were what appeared to be bureaucratic workers. They sat at desks within triangular spaces with heaps of papers around them as they frantically attempted to sort them into various piles. The bots took me up an escalator and as I reached a higher floor I looked down at the atrium below me. A series of walls surrounded the Burc offices which had small openings that led to narrow corridors. The scene reminded me of a game children long ago played where one held a labyrinth-like puzzle and tried to move a tiny silver ball through the maze.

The bots took me to a chamber that had no windows. It, too, was in the shape of a triangle with a stone table similarly shaped. The walls consisted of a dark gray steel. There were video monitors sitting on the table. The bots had me sit in a chair at the base of the geometric form. Aside from the noise produced by the ventilation system, the room was quiet. A door along the edge of one side of the room hissed open and Lask entered. I started to rise but he motioned that I should stay seated. He sat at a chair along the side of the table that did not have a monitor in front of it.

The screens, which had been dark, now turned on and Burcs were on display on each of the screens. They wore clothing similar to Lask's simple attire. Since there were eight of them, plus Lask, I assumed that this was a virtual meeting with the Procs. The individual at the point of the table did not introduce himself as the Top Proc, but instead had a sign under him that read "One." I knew he was the leader since he spoke first and his hunched-over appearance and weak voice reflected his ill health.

"We are here to see what to do with you. You may not be what we thought. Lask said you could be a Syntharmian, and you may know of the Domandosemprians. We have learned that you may have lied to your host."

I looked at Lask, who ignored my glance.

"We have heard that you told Og that you are from a place called Earth," continued One, "Lask's son, Pots, told his mate to be, Tar, of your home. Tar heard from Pots that you filled Og's mind with strange, wrong thoughts that could harm our way of life. Speak if this charge is true!"

I again glanced at Lask, who still gave me no hint of what to do. If I lied and tried to continue the fallacy that I was a Syntharmian, Lask and his children might be in jeopardy if I did not try to distance myself from them. I decided to admit that I was from Earth, and had perpetuated Lask's assumption during interrogation that I was a Syntharmian who had information about the Domandosemprians. I stated I only responded to Og's questions because they arose out of normal curiosity.

"To ask too much is to start the ruin of who we are," said the female Proc known as Five. "Why did you not keep with our ways?"

Since my interference here was already a fact, I decided to make the best argument I could. I said that I answered Og's questions to discourage wild speculation, which I stressed would go against the Burc Code. I resolved to speak about the positive aspects of curious inquiry. I noted on Earth that there was a desire to understand how natural phenomena worked, and to gather more knowledge about the environment, including plant and animal life along with the weather to learn how to better the ecosystem. I exalted scientific exploration which led to modern inventions such as the computer to make it easier to process data and discover more about the workings of the universe. I praised philosophical arguments that furthered the quest for an ultimate understanding of the nature and purpose of existence.

"Here, a Burc can't choose," I stressed. "They are told what they must do and be. They may not look at the skies and find out what is there and ask why they are here. They do not use their free thoughts to make their lives feel whole. Their minds are in jail."

After a pause, number Three asked, "But does your kind lead lives of joy with no fear?"

The question surprised me, and put me on pause. Even though on Earth there were many liberties, that fact did not necessarily translate to making individuals happy or safe. People certainly experienced periods of "joy," when they fell in love, had children, laughed together and enjoyed their work. But weren't their lives full of stress, dread, and unfulfillment? Wasn't there a great deal of anger, and didn't people in large numbers take drugs to seek escape. Wasn't there a significant number of suicides?

"I see by your lack of speech that your way is not as good as you would like us to think," said Three.

"The Gens knew the pain of too much thought," said Five. "Why ask so much if it leaves one sad, hurt, lost. There is no point to life but to eat, drink, breathe, sleep, and give birth to more of one's kind. The rest is more than we need, and brings pain."

The Procs looked at One who coughed and his eyes drooped. His breathing was raspy.

"It is felt that you are a threat to us," he said. "We can't trust that you are not a spy for our foes. If all say yes, we must give you the Cure, make you our spy, and send you to Domandosempria."

I was frightened and tried to argue against the dreaded treatment.

"I can help you with your fight as I am. I have learned so much about Burc and that will aid me in my quest to help you end your war," I pleaded.

But the Group's distrust of me prevailed. Their vote seconded the opinion of the Top Proc. Lask sided with the other Procs, which at first shocked me. He wanted me to go to the other planet, not as an informant, but as a diplomat, and with my mind intact. But I hoped that he was just faking a show of unity, and had some other plan. Guards took me to a small, dark cell in the lower levels of the building, and secured me there. The room was heavy with dampness. It seemed that despite my efforts to escape my confinement on Earth that held my invention and my person as a prisoner that I continued to find myself locked away.

My jail had the basic components of any place of incarceration on Earth. There was a cot to sleep on, a sink, a toilet, and a slot in the door for the delivery of food. The only light came from a small window in the wall that was close to the ceiling so that I could not view anything. As I sat on my stiff mattress, I realized that this type of imprisonment produced just the opposite effect of what Burc society advocated. I had nothing to divert me, nothing that stopped me from thinking. I thought about how I left my home planet, which I felt had become so lethal in its violence toward its own people, hoping for a different place that fostered a sense of family and community among its inhabitants. But, to reach that end, the individuals here could not think for themselves, make choices about what they wanted out of existence, or solve the mysteries of the cosmos.

I was in the cell for several days, and used the only tool I had at my disposal, my mind. I passed the time by reviewing the arguments of John Locke and wondered if the Burcs would have embraced his beliefs in selfish utilitarianism and the idea that the mind is a blank slate on which others could imprint preferred behavior. They would probably agree with him, given how extreme was the control over their society. Through their actions, the Burcs subscribed to the idea that any desire to utilize the individual's extra brain capacity, beyond applying it to essentials for survival, could be circumscribed through conditioning, the way Ivan Pavlov influenced the behavior of his dogs.

I understood the relief from mental anguish that derived from such a plan on how to live. But, wasn't there some higher purpose to life, or else why did we have the drive to question and explore? Was it part of some grand design that spurred us on to burst out of the contentment derived from restricted mental activities? Or did our insatiable intellectual quests result from a freak evolutionary development that left sentient beings with more gray matter than necessary?

I tried to stop thinking about philosophical questions, and changed the channel in my head to thoughts about some of my favorite books. I mentally flipped through the titles of several of my preferred readings. I conjured up passages from *1984*, *Brave New World*, and *Moby Dick*. Although entertaining, it seemed as if my choices in literature fed the flames of my burning desire to reflect upon the questions that life posed, and I felt no relief.

Chapter Thirteen

My brain exhausted, I finally fell asleep, but it was a fitful rest, as I had nightmares of experiencing the Cure, which my unconscious mind depicted as a beam of light erasing line by line all my memories. I then found myself not remembering who I was and where I came from, But, this panic was temporary as the Burcs filled the void with precepts of The Code. They then ordered me to clean windows and then dirty them afterwards, and I had to repeat the task over and over again.

My troubled rest ended when an alarm rang. Lights in the cell and outside in the corridor repeatedly flashed brighter and then dimmer. I heard running in the corridor outside my cell. I smelled the harsh odor of something burning and panic seized me. I began to sweat and breathe quickly. What if there was a fire and I was left here to die? I rallied my hope since the Procs would want me alive to carry out their plans for me to infiltrate their enemy. My conclusion was valid since two bots opened the door to my cell, grabbed me, put an oxygen supplement hood on my head, and rushed me through the smoke-filled hallway.

The bots took me outside the Hub, and Lask was there, waiting. He said nothing and we all entered the same type of tram that brought me to the building. After a silent ride the tram stopped, and when I left the vehicle I found myself back at Lask's hut. We entered the building and went to my room. The bots stationed themselves on either side of the doorway. Lask had one of his short wands with him. He pressed a couple of buttons, the bots uttered mechanical sounds, and then left the room. I assumed Lask had initiated some form of override to allow us to be alone.

"You lit the fire," I said to him.

He nodded.

"I spoke to the Top Proc as the fire grew and told him that to save the plan to send you as a spy, I would get you out of the Hub and keep you here. But, the Cure is to take place soon. You must get to your ship and leave. I know I asked for your help, but the risk may be too great for you. You must leave to be safe, to a place not Domandosempria, if you wish."

Lask's caring about my welfare moved me. He may have placed himself in danger if the Procs discovered his actions to rescue me.

"What will you tell the Procs if I can't be found? They will blame you, and they might give you the Cure."

"I have thought of that," he said. "But I will say you stole one of my wands, learned how to use it, and used the bot guards to help you leave. You left at night while we slept. So, no one can see me with you as you go to your ship."

He searched in his robe and pulled out a wand and handed it to me.

"If you come back to Burc, press here. We can talk through it so I can help you."

I told him I was grateful for all he had done for me. We gathered my belongings, and he asked if I would be returning to Earth.

"No," I said. "There is no life for me there right now. I have a debt to pay, and a job to do. I will go to Domandosempria, as you asked."

Chapter Fourteen

Lask gave me the coordinates to reach Domandosempria. He programmed a bot to take me to my ship. In my backpack that I brought from the Seeker I used a light beacon to avoid sinkholes and areas of quicksand. I used the GPS application that linked my wristwatch to the transducer to locate where I hid the device under some rocks on the other side of the plateau where I landed the Seeker. I found my spacecraft in good condition, unmolested, as Lask promised. I hooked up the transducer to the HOPS and entered the settings to take me to Domandosempria. I first had to fly high above the ground to safely engage the propulsion system without atmospheric resistance. I fired the thruster engines. I began to rise off the surface and headed towards the upper atmosphere.

As I was ready to reach orbit around the planet, several of the figure-eight spacecraft were approaching. One of the Domandosemprian ships veered toward me. The other ships drew closer to the planet and began to fire on the ground below. The Burc defenses were already aware of their approach and fired back. The craft that focused on me seemed more exploratory than hostile, as the occupants probably wondered what the Seeker was, since it was an unfamiliar ship. However, when I attempted to put some distance between myself and it, the alien ship began to fire its white light blasters at the Seeker. I was able to maneuver my craft away from these initial attacks, but worried that a concerted effort by the Domandosemprian vessel would eventually hit its mark. I weaved around the light shafts, barely evading the burst of brilliant beams. I initiated the HOPS just in time to rocket away as a flash of whiteness was about to overtake me.

I again experienced the vibrating and blurring of the inside of the ship. Despite my prior experience, I was still frightened by the feeling of the loss of reality as the shape of the ship changed. As before, I felt an overwhelming nausea at the compression of my body as the Seeker rocketed like a subatomic particle in an accelerator. Once more I experienced rapidly changing visions, this time of a long tunnel with question marks inside. The interrogative symbols appeared in my mind as if they were painted along the walls of the elongated enclosure. I saw my arms reaching for the curly tails of the markings, but they began to move and squirm away. I finally grabbed the largest question mark there. As I did so, it seemed to turn into the capital "U" seated on a straight line that forked at the bottom, the same carving which I saw on the outside of The Safe. Then I blacked out.

Part Two

DomandoSempria

Chapter Fifteen

The Seeker converted back into stable matter form and I began to recover from the effects of the HOPS drive. My nausea continued for a longer period this time and I vomited once. I also felt fatigued, as if the trip drained my body's strength. However, my mind was quite alert as I immediately noticed a red warning light blinking, as if flirting for my attention. The signal alerted me that there was something wrong with the life support system. A look at the exterior camera viewing screens showed the craft was venting oxygen into space. I would have to eventually find the leak so I could travel again. I placed my helmet on to utilize the auxiliary oxygen in my suit's supply. I saw Domandosempria before me on the main viewer. It was significantly smaller than Burc. I accessed the ship's navigational assistance system and used the magnification control to find a landing spot. I chose one of the coordinates that the computer suggested for touchdown which was a manageable hiking distance to an area that the organic assessment program deemed a populated area.

I was anxious about encountering another alien species, unsure of how they would perceive me. But, I was also curious as to how these people lived after hearing the stories about them on Burc. In addition, I had a mission, which gave me a sense of purpose. If there was any way that I could aid in ending hostilities between the two planets then I would feel fulfilled in achieving a worthy goal.

Just as was the case with Burc, the atmosphere on this planet was similar to that on earth, but here there was an abundance of life-sustaining elements in the air so there was no need for a supplemental breathing apparatus. After I powered down the Seeker's systems, I exited the spaceship. The burning star that acted as a sun was larger here than the one near Burc, and even surpassed the size of the one in Earth's solar system. Its brightness flamed illumination throughout the planet's sky. I surveyed the scenery and found the land was lush with greenery. I saw aircraft that looked like small drones hovering over the trees and rainbow-colored flowers. They sprayed what I assumed was irrigating fluid over the vegetation. As I started to walk, I felt a pronounced difference in locomotion from what I experienced on Burc. Here, due to the decreased gravity, if I pushed my feet off the ground, I launched myself a couple of feet from the surface. I was feeling stronger and was grateful for this change since it helped compensate for some lingering muscle strain from being on Burc.

I again removed the transducer and buried it near the roots of a tree with blue leaves. I activated the homing device on it and synced it with my wristwatch's GPS application. I began the walk to the edge of the inhabited place the ship picked up on its sensors. I was surprised to see some objects approach me that turned out to be types of hovercrafts. When they arrived at my location several robots sprang from the vehicles and grabbed me by the arms and legs. As they carried me to one of the hovercrafts, I screamed at them to let me go. One of the androids fastened my arms and legs with metallic restraints. Another used an armlike appendage to measure the size of my head (the robot had a rather large metallic cranium). They did not use language to communicate so I assumed they must be using some form of wireless electronic means to coordinate their actions. I squirmed and yelled, but they ignored me. I felt panic grip me, worrying that they concluded I was a Burc. I feared they might torture me for information, and then kill me.

The additional hovercraft approached and I hoped they would contain organic life forms so I could plead with them that I meant no harm. There were indeed nonmechanical creatures onboard these vehicles. They exited their hovercrafts and walked toward me, stopping several yards from where I stood. They surveyed me and the Seeker. These beings were comparable in height to humans on Earth, but their heads were larger. There must have been about two dozen aliens who eventually left their vehicles. A few approached me and I assumed they were younger Domandosemprians since they had dark hair and smooth skin. The others which I classified as being older, with wrinkled skin, larger noses and ears, and grey hair, stayed farther back. As opposed to the numerous layers of clothes worn by the Burcs, these inhabitants dressed in a minimal amount of apparel. Many wore tunics of various colors, and some of the younger ones wore skimpy outfits that displayed a great deal of their bodies. The females appeared to have breasts for nursing and wider hips for delivering babies, similar to women on Earth. All of them looked at me up and down and began to speak to each other as they circled me. As I listened to their conversation, I found that there were fewer breaks between words, indicating a polysyllabic language. The rising tones at the end of each speech segment sounded as if they were asking questions. The individuals became quite loud as they talked to each other, with some interrupting the conversations of the others.

"I come in peace. I mean you no harm," I said in English, since speaking Burc would not be a winning move. There was one in the group, an individual wearing a blue tunic and who appeared slender and tall, close to six feet, two inches in height, approached me. Since there were limited amounts of gray hair on his head I judged that he was middle-aged, but was not sure what that meant on this planet. Those on Burc had a slightly shorter life span than the average inhabitant of Earth I eventually learned. He handed me an ear bud. After inserting it, I was shocked to find that the device translated what those present were saying into my native tongue.

"Where have you traveled?" asked one.

"How old are you?" said another.

"What is your name?" said a third.

"We at first thought you were a Syntharmian," another said.

"What is the source of your spacecraft's fuel?" one asked.

There followed a cacophony of interrogatives, and the middle-aged man told the others to quiet down. He then gave some sort of cryptic command to the robots that restrained me. The only word I heard was "override." One of the robots then released me from my bonds.

"My name is Definimos," he said. "I apologize for the verbal onslaught of my companions. We have a tendency to ask questions first and, again, ask questions later. Your appearance intrigues us, as does your spacecraft. We desire to know as much about you as possible."

I decided to go native and ask a question of my own.

"My name is Samuel Galloper. How do you know my language?"

Definimos smiled, as did the others, before he answered.

"Oh, we don't. Our translator reads your sounds and converts them to our language. Once you spoke, the programming generated commonalities of word tones between our respective speech patterns. It may have a bit of a delay sometimes, and there may be some variances. We have visited some planets within our traveling range, and others we have electronically monitored. We studied the occupants of those planets, and programmed their languages into our planet-wide system to which the ear devices connect remotely. That is the reason why we can understand each other. Many of us have learned the various languages we have encountered. We are always practicing the tongues of others. The earbud facilitates that practice while still allowing those with no knowledge of our words to comprehend the speaker in our native language. There have been many studies to seek out which language is the most effective. We are quite the talkers and readers, so we delight in linguistics."

"What were the results of your studies?" I asked.

"They have been inconclusive so far," said Definimos. "But the inquiry is ongoing. When we first saw you we hypothesized that you may be a Syntharmian, since your head and body dimensions seem to fit what legend has indicated about that race, even though we have not encountered them. What we do know has been open to speculation. Does that answer your question?"

"Yes, quite extensively," I said. "I must compliment you on your linguistic endeavors."

"Oh, why thank you," said Definimos as he bowed.

"What type of food does he like to eat?" asked one of the others there.

"What is your purpose here?" asked a second.

"Ask him how he was able to travel here?" said another.

"All of you be quiet, please!" said Definimos. "Our people can be a bit overwhelming. But, we are very interested as to how you journeyed through the cosmos to arrive here."

I was not about to divulge anything about the HOPS to these strangers, who were waging war with others.

"It was a fluke," I said. "I am from a planet called Earth and I speak a language called English. I was exploring my solar system and I inadvertently discovered a wormhole. The phenomena dragged me into it, and I wound up here. But, it appears that my ship's oxygen containment system has become damaged."

Definimos gave me a sideways glance as if he found my explanation dubious. But then he smiled.

"I am a temporary member of the Governing Brain Trust here. Well, everything is sort of temporary around here," he said as he looked around and the others chuckled. I wondered what that comment meant. It sounded upsetting to me, conveying the possibility of chaos. Or was it a general statement about the fragility of life? In any event, the Domandosemprians did not see anything upsetting about the comment, and I was curious as to why they seemed at home with instability.

"In any event, why don't you accompany me, and you can rest, eat, and especially talk about your travels. Oh, and we'll have our mechanicals transport your spacecraft for diagnostic testing and they will effectuate repairs of any of its defects."

"Well, I'm not so sure that is advisable ..." I said, alarmed at what they might discover about the Seeker.

"Oh no, we love investigating how things work," said Definimos. "We actually are delighted to have something new to ponder."

I didn't want to arouse suspicion, so I didn't protest, hoping it would take quite a while before the Domandosemprians would learn about the propulsion system. But from what I had already observed, they would have numerous questions for me. I hopped in one of the hover vehicles at Definimos's invitation and we headed toward the nearby metropolis.

After our ride we exited our hovercrafts and I looked around and saw a very modern city, with skyscrapers and skywalks. The buildings, through some sort of advanced engineering, looked like inverted pyramids, with the sides extending outward from a much smaller flat base which allowed visitors to enter. The entryways were broad at the top and narrowed at the base. People seemed to prefer wandering above the ground than on it, since there were fewer people on the streets than on the open walkways between buildings. There were exterior glass-enclosed elevators rising and descending on the sides of the buildings. Numerous "mechanicals" scurried about the exterior of the edifices, moving like metallic insects. They were cleaning the streets, going into manholes, climbing up auxiliary poles, and even scaling the sides of the buildings. They reminded me of the robots in the film version of Isaac Asimov's *I, Robot*, except these had no facial characteristics. In that way, they were more like Gort, the animatron from *The Day the Earth Stood Still*. My mother loved science fiction films, and that passion filtered down to me. The thought of her warmed me on one hand but also made me ache for her loss.

"I see you have observed our numerous mechanical helpers scampering back and forth and up and down," said Definimos. "They are implementing repairs and providing routine maintenance. In fact, we are almost completely automated here. They take care of all the busy jobs that would otherwise bog our citizens down."

Definimos hesitated before speaking again, and the tone of his voice became lower, as if he was stressing a serious matter.

"The mechanicals are also very useful in repairing the destruction unleashed during our war with another planet."

I felt I wanted to have that discussion later, after I established more trust with my new host.

"I noticed that there is no attempt to make the mechanicals appear like organic life forms," I said. "Don't you want to interact with them on a personal level?"

"We created these worker units for practical, not intellectual pursuits. They construct buildings, perform maintenance on power systems, and repair operational defects. In fact, there are mechanicals that just fix other mechanicals. I dare say that we wouldn't know what to do if they ceased to function."

"Couldn't that be a problem?" I asked. "Suppose you had a massive power outage."

"Hasn't happened yet. Besides, we have numerous backup energy sources, including solar and thermal, so we don't have to be bothered. You do seem preoccupied with details, aren't you?" said the smiling Definimos.

I decided to shift gears.

"You said you don't use these artificial intelligence units for mental pursuits. What about scientific explorations and other academic disciplines?"

"Oh, we employ various mechanicals for evidence and data gathering. We also have higher functioning cerebral synthetics to help us explore the philosophical and scientific mysteries of the galaxy. And, we have ones that live with our families that function as android companions that perform domestic functions and aid in intellectual pursuits. These last two groups have faces that somewhat resemble ours. Come with me and I will show you where I live, at least for now."

Chapter Sixteen

We entered one of the inverted buildings and rode the escalator to the top floor. After we ascended, I observed that many of the natives were on the protruding part of the roof that acted like a balcony to view the city. Some were conversing with each other, while many sat motionless as if in a trance, perhaps listening to the voices in their heads. Still more stood still at the edges of the buildings, which had no protective barriers, staring off into the distance.

"This sector of the planet is called Darnounoby," said Definimos. "It is the largest community on Domandosempria, with a little over ten million occupants. Although each community has its own evolving government, there is constant communication and visitation between the various habitats."

"Is it safe for those so close to the edge of the building?" I asked Definimos, my concern distracting me from his orientation speech. "It looks quite dangerous."

"We do not believe in barriers," said my host. "Unfortunately, it is true that some of the citizens have fallen off. One of the tradeoffs for our way of life."

"Is totally unrestricted freedom worth it if part of the bargain involves the needless deaths of individuals?" I asked, feeling that some philosophical stands may be too extreme.

Definimos nodded his head as he closed his eyes. "The accidents have been increasing at alarming rates," he said. "I am concerned that our inability to compromise our belief that there should be no limitations has put us in jeopardy."

The adults here on average were taller than those on Earth, about six feet, two inches to four inches in height. I wondered what genetic trait caused them all to have eyes that featured various shades of grey. We entered Definimos's home, which was sprawling, taking up most of the top of the building. Large windows wrapped around its perimeter.

The living room area contained several reclining chairs and sofas which were of differing sizes and shapes, all of which seemed to be stuffed with some sort of fluffy material that made the scene look like a pillow factory had exploded there. The walls were decorated in various colors, some bright, some subdued, and there were multiple shades of reds, blues, whites, black, and especially grays The most remarkable aspect of the abode was that the floor and ceiling were transparent. Since the residence was on the top floor, there was an amazing view of the heavens above. It was an exhilarating sensation as I felt I could almost touch the universe with my eyes and mind. However, those living below could see into Definimos's home, and vice versa.

"You don't have much privacy here," was my obvious observation.

"Privacy is just another wall that separates us from knowing more about others, and, thus, that which is beyond us, and our limited bodies," said Definimos. "However, my family does not offer a view of our bathrooms and bedrooms. Even for us, the observing looks of others might cause an inhibition as to how we uniquely express our nakedness, which would be counterproductive to the primacy of the individual."

He hesitated.

"You seem disconcerted. Am I correct in assuming that your culture would find this openness quite alien?"

"Yes," I said. "Most of us tend to value our seclusion. I know I do, when it is by my choice. While I was doing my scientific experiments I was under constant observation by military superiors. I guess it makes me feel safe not to be scrutinized. When others observe me, I suppose, it can become intimidating."

"Let me assure you, dear Samuel, that there is no centralized, autocratic government with an agenda peering into our lives to control us here." He laughed. "We have so many disparate views on almost everything that we can just about agree on when to eat dinner."

Sitting on three of the different recliners were two girls and one boy that appeared to be between about seven and eleven years of age. As soon as they saw us they came running toward me, asking questions. Definimos interrupted them.

"Please access your translator devices, children, so that you can understand what our guest has to say," said Definimos. "This visitor is from a distant planet called Earth. This is my daughter Infinisia, her sister Thomasina, and our visiting child, Hypothico. This is Samuel Galloper."

The youngsters inserted their earbuds and wasted no time interrogating me, just as those I met earlier.

"Why have you left your planet?" asked Inifinisia, her brown eyes wide open, looking like an intellectual vacuum cleaner.

"Why did you choose to visit our home?" asked Thomasina, with squinting eyes and a head tilting toward suspicion.

"What do you believe are the origins of the universe?" said Hypothico.

I felt my face recoil from the onslaught of questions and took a quick gulp of air. I felt inundated by a sea of possible responses. Definimos rescued me.

"I admire your inquisitiveness, children," he said. "But Samuel has just arrived and has not yet adapted to our mode of existence. I am sure he will be willing to answer your questions later. For now, why don't you have some fun returning to your metaphysics applications."

This suggestion seemed an odd one to me to divert children, but it did appear to placate them. They went to their individual seats, bouncing on them as they settled in, and started generating holographic images from small digital tablets in front of them. Thomasina turned to address me.

"We will want to know everything about you," she said.

I smiled but hid my worry inside, afraid of what might happen to me if they knew that I came as an emissary from Burc. I continued to wear my pasted grin as Definimos led me to a doorless, but secluded corner of the floor to his study.

"Hypothico is here for a semester. We Domandosemprians wish our youths to experience many viewpoints. So, our youngsters rotate among other families with children that attend the same schools. During the next school session, we will have another offspring from other parents living with us, and Hypothico will rejoin his family. And, Thomasina will live with a schoolmate's family for the semester."

My response was to shake my head in disapproval. "Doesn't that create confusion among the children?" I said. "I guess I'm wondering if they have problems reconnecting with their parents, who should be special to them, once they return home. Do the children have difficulty knowing where to invest their love?"

"Confusion can be the impetus for discovery," Definimos said. "Besides, spreading our love among many is preferable to concentrating on just a few. It encourages a universal attitude of caring for all."

I decided not to argue this point further, because I started to feel conflicted. I thought about children I encountered on Earth who appeared brainwashed into believing that their parents' racial and political ideas were absolute. It looked like Definimos saw that I was troubled.

"We can continue this discussion later. By the way, my spousal will be home a bit later," said Definimos. "Her name is Pansapianna, and she currently is involved in a project to determine if the laws of thermodynamics can be broken."

I felt myself raise my eyebrows in a display of surprise. "Can that possibly be?" I asked. "I mean, aren't those laws constant?"

Definimos gave a slight smile and shook his head, almost in resignation. "Nothing seems to be constant," he said. "Except, apparently, war, which tends to go on forever. Change is a healthier state of being."

A thought came to me since we were discussing families.

"Do you also rotate spousals?" I asked, using the translated equivalent of the native language word.

"It's totally voluntary since adults consent to their own arrangements," he said. "Some have polyamorous marriages, and others engage in multiple sexual encounters."

"I can see how exploring sexual boundaries can be interesting," I said, my mind picturing erotic situations and becoming somewhat aroused. "But, from my perspective, I can again see having confusing emotions. We on Earth, for the most part, have not been able to overcome envy and jealousy. Maybe we shouldn't. Devoting yourself to someone makes the relationship special, more intimate."

"We come to our own conclusions in the matter," said Definimos. "Pansapianna and I agree with your idea about exclusiveness. We have found that a monogamous relationship suits our personalities. Have you been married?"

The question stopped me in my conversational tracks. I was always reluctant to discuss my amorous encounters with others. I felt embarrassed by my lack of success in this area.

"No, I have not," I said in a Burc manner.

Definimos was not satisfied. "Come now, you must elaborate," he said. "We are developing an interpersonal connection, and for it to grow we must both nourish it with our contributions."

I did not want to have anything stand in the way of learning more about this world, so I reluctantly indulged my host.

"I have had a number of intimate connections with others," I said slowly. "But, I realized I selfishly used them as temporary distractions to give me relief from my driven pursuit of scientific knowledge. My focused intellectual pursuits have not allowed me to be able, thus far, to enjoy deeply connecting with another."

"It appears that your insatiable scientific mind shows how you are similar to Domandosemprians," said Definimos.

"It would appear so," I agreed. "But, you do have a spousal and children."

"We have learned for the good of the whole that we must mate and procreate and guide offspring toward individual intellectual exploration," said Definimos. "Do you at least have friends?"

"Some," I replied. "My best friend is my brother, Arthur."

"And yet," said Definimos, "you left him behind."

"Yes," I said and I felt sad. "I guess I have a way to go to learn about true caring for others."

"May I ask, does your brother have an area of expertise, or does he dabble in many areas of study?" he asked.

"He is a fiction writer," I said.

"Interesting," said Definimos. "The two of you represent discovery and imagination. These two aspects are related, as are you and Arthur. They both can break boundaries."

"Well, I guess I have been writing lately, also. Nonfiction, since I have been recording my journey in a log, and adding my take on experiences," I said.

The smile on Definimos's face widened so much that I thought it would wrap around his large head.

"Marvelous!" he said.

Definimos offered me a slice of what looked like chiffon pie since it was so light and fluffy, but it was not a dessert, as it had a savory taste. The liquid I drank was orange in color, and it was sweet and frothy. After several gulps I began to feel a bit buzzed. I became somewhat alarmed, and I asked what caused this effect.

"Do not be concerned," Definimos said after laughing. "It is a fermented fruit. You might become mildly intoxicated. Not sure how it will affect your anatomy, but then all of existence is an experiment, isn't it? We do, however, have mind altering substances here that allow for the expansion of awareness, unfortunately only temporarily."

After we had finished our snack, I asked why Definimos said that this place was only an interim home.

"Well, let's face it, everything is transitory," he said. "But, more specifically, as I believe I mentioned, I am, for the time being, whatever that time may be, a member of the Governing Brain Trust that oversees the happenings of this sector. This housing is for someone in that office. We don't really have immutable laws or rules on Domandosempria. And as I noted, there is no one central government. Each sector democratically decides how to run things in its area. Members of the committees just make sure that whatever the guidelines are in place at the time, are, more or less, adhered to. There are changes to those rules quite often, since life is so mutable. There are virtual meetings that join those of all areas when it comes to defending the planet as a whole from outside aggression or environmental concerns that could threaten all of us at the same time."

"When do you have elections? Are there set terms for the Trust's members? How are laws enacted and changed?" I felt wobbly due to the drink but also about all this uncertainty after living with the social fortifications that solidified life on Burc.

"It is wonderful that you have an inquisitive mind," commented Definimos. "But, again, you focus on practical particulars. Citizens or members of the Trust introduce proposed changes to our lives, and the population votes and the majority determines whether to enact or dismiss the changes. Whenever a Trust member feels like doing something else, he just does. Or, if the population, on its own, by a majority, decides they want a change, they vote for a new individual, or two, or seven, that number being the maximum serving on the Trust."

"It seems to me unnerving, not knowing where you will call home at any time," I said. My military training was rejecting an attempt to graft uncertainty onto my programmed synapses.

"Not for us. We see it as a way to explore new experiences. All our people swap places whenever they feel the need to overcome inertia and they find others willing to make the switch."

"It sounds exhausting, moving all of one's stuff about so much," I argued.

"We don't usually take very many of our old belongings to the next experience," said Definimos. "We try not to emphasize personal property. Bringing old baggage forward can act as an anchor, inhibiting exploration. We enjoy how the new surroundings and its previous owners' objects will provide us with a refreshed way of living,"

My wobbly sensation gave way to dizziness, and I had to sit onto one of the puffy chairs which provided as much support as a cloud.

"My, you look a bit unmoored, which usually isn't such a bad thing," observed Definimos. "But you do not seem to be handling it well. Why don't you lie down and rest a bit. We can talk later."

I gratefully agreed and began to drift off, pushed into my unconscious sea by what I encountered so far, and no doubt, by that orange drink I consumed. I awoke feeling better. I found Definimos sitting near me engrossed by what he was looking at on a slender digital tablet. He noticed my arousal.

"Feeling better, I hope?"

I pointed to the tablet.

"Interesting?" I asked.

"Yes, indeed," said Definimos. "One of our groups is exploring the theory whose premise is that we are already dead. And if so, what was our form prior to this one, and what would the next mode of existence be, when we die in this state. What do you think?"

Not knowing how to respond to such a question, I offered, "I would have to think about that one."

"Precisely!" said Definimos.

Chapter Seventeen

I had a chance to wash up in an automated bathroom, where a schematic instructed that all I had to do was press buttons next to illustrations of water and soap which then flowed from the sides of a basin. I cleaned my hands and face, and then hot air blew through vents situated in the silver wall in front of me, drying me off. After feeling refreshed, I was surprised that Definimos asked if I would like to take a walk around the city of Darnounoby.

"I don't have to wear a disguise? My appearance will not upset your people?" I asked.

"Absolutely not," said Definimos. "Quite the opposite, as you have already seen. In fact we have a saying here. I wonder if the translator comes up with a version in your language that would make sense. It's, 'Curiosity feeds the regit.' A regit is an animal here. It lives in jungle areas and has claws, sharp teeth and six legs. Does the phrase hold any meaning for you?"

"It is sort of a reversal of our saying, but I understand what you mean," I replied.

After a pause I said to Definimos, "I am curious as to what other positions you have held in your society."

"I have been an advanced mathematics instructor," said Definimos. "My class once made some breakthroughs concerning variations of arithmetic definitions. We explored the flexibility of mathematical postulates. For instance, two plus two doesn't always require the sum of four. If the answer is three, we could then alter other calculations to fit the pattern."

I shook my head in disapproval. "How can you maintain consistency in your methods by changing basic rules of computation?" I said. "How would that be practical?"

"Oh, it isn't practical at all, but it is fascinating contemplating the possibilities," said Definimos. "I have also been a music teacher. Our free-form compositions consist of a random pattern approach."

"On my world, that would come under the musical category that we call jazz," I said.

"Fascinating," said Definimos, and he seemed elated by this fact. "And, I have dabbled in painting and have been a curator of an art museum. I have a copy of one of my efforts on my imager. We are interested in abstract depictions that do not follow any rules concerning lines, colors, or subjects."

Definimos handed me a device that was similar to a tablet and I looked at a painting that reminded me of a Jackson Pollock composition. I smiled, thinking that many on Earth who have seen Pollock's works would believe he was really an alien.

"I feel as if I am just beginning to explore other occupations and hope to experience recreating myself in various intellectual forms," said Definimos.

"May I ask how old you are?" I said.

"Why of course," said Definimos. "I am one hundred and five units. Our average lifespan here is about two hundred and seventeen. We measure our cycles by the rotation around our star, as most civilizations do. We have extended our lifespans with medical advances so that we can have a longer time to continue our explorations."

After I calculated time on Earth versus that on Domandosempria, I confirmed that these inhabitants lived approximately seventy years longer than those on Earth. I was envious of the extended time that the Domadosemprians were able to exist and was quiet for a bit as I thought about all I could achieve if I lived longer. I wanted to further explore the cosmos. I hungered to discover how existence and its creatures came to be. There was still so much to learn.

These thoughts again brought me back to memories of my mother. I became a scientist because I am my mother's son. She always asked me questions as I grew up. "If you throw a ball up in the air while in a boat, why does that object drop down into your hands instead of landing in the water behind you?' Or, "Do objects fall at the same speed?" She explained to me about vectors and gravitational acceleration. I felt satisfied when she revealed her knowledge of how the physical world worked. I was thrilled when she gave me my first holographic virtual reality set, which helped me view phenomena from all sides. But, I began to have questions about the purpose of existence, that neither my mother, nor later, professors could answer. I felt lost in that place of uncertainty. It was like traveling in a dangerous fog.

My mind was among the stars as we descended to a floor where one of the skywalks connected the building to another. The path through the open-air passage allowed one the ability to see as far as the eye could envision. The sky was clear with wispy clouds slowly creeping in the wind. There were floating mechanical devices levitating about. I asked what was their purpose.

"I am so happy to be able to have someone with an inquisitive mind to join me," said Definimos. "Well, we have learned how to alter the weather to a degree. We can introduce catalysts to create rain to grow crops and wind to help with pollination. We can dissipate severe storm fronts that cause damaging wind formations. We preserve warm and cold seasons to maintain variety. Otherwise, it would be quite boring with the same climate all the time, wouldn't you agree?"

"How did you obtain this ability?" I asked, shaking my head in wonderment.

"Well. much the same way you came to be here, I suppose. Always investigating, hypothesizing, experimenting. The mechanicals do the labor and some of them help with the theorizing."

As we walked, I observed various animals moving about. Some were bird-like, and either strolled along the concourse or took flight. There were also four-legged creatures with fur, and which had squinty eyes and long snouts. Their sizes ranged from the length of a cocker spaniel to that of a German Shepherd.

"You seem to have a problem with unsheltered animals here," I commented.

"Not at all!" said Definimos. "We prefer not to cage our feathered and furry friends. We feed and care for them in the open, and provide shelter when necessary."

There were numerous Domandosemprians walking on these bridges in the air. Several were looking at holographic images like the ones that Definimos's children generated. A few began to notice me, and they woke up from their mental immersions. They first stared, then approached us. Definimos told them of the language difference and those who were not wearing the translator earbuds inserted them. They then began playing way more than Twenty Questions with me. They asked everything from how old I was, and what color I liked, to how long is the gestation period for a fetus on my planet and what is the average lifespan on Earth. One male wanted to know what the most serious problem was facing my planet. The answer for me was easy.

"Trying to stop wars and maintain peace," I said.

I thought this answer would meet with unified agreement. I was wrong.

"We must never allow enemies to take away freedoms!" yelled one citizen.

"Yes, the Burcs would turn us all into low-level mechanicals!" shouted another.

"But, there have been too many casualties," said a third. "How do we win without so much loss?"

"We must find new ways to fight for our way of life," said another individual.

The back and forth among the citizens continued.

"Let's analyze and synthesize various proposals of war and peace."

"What is war and peace? Of what elements do they truly consist?"

Many more Domandosemprians joined the debate until there was a huge orchestra of various opinionated sections, each playing its own tune, without a unifying melody.

I looked at Definimos, who just shrugged, and led me away from the crowd.

"This type of interchange happens all of the time," he said. "Some will be fortified by their views, others will completely change how they think, some will walk away disenchanted. As long as there is an exchange of ideas we mostly seem content."

He paused.

"I believe what you said is logical," he said. "How can anyone feel free when war threatens to obliterate the individual experience of existence?"

After hearing his words, I became hopeful that Definimos might be the right person to approach on Lask's behalf. But, I stifled my enthusiasm, since I had just arrived here, and needed, like a good scientist, to gather more data about these inhabitants, and especially about Definimos, before possibly jeopardizing my mission and myself.

My host guided me to a building where Domandosemprians stood in front of an outside shop counter. There were a couple of individuals eating what looked like ice cream. Definimos ushered me inside.

"You must try some of our frozen desserts. As you can see, we have many flavors to choose from."

He pointed to a wall where there was a digital readout of hundreds of possibilities. The customers were engrossed in discussions about the various flavors. When I asked Definimos why hardly anyone was eating, several of the people there used their earbuds so they could communicate with me.

"You are a visitor? How have you come to be here," asked one male. "Will you be staying long? What do your people believe about the origins of the galaxy?"

Definimos interrupted and addressed one of the male customers.

"Have you decided on a choice and why have you come to that conclusion?"

The customer pondered.

"I have narrowed it down to ten flavors," he said. "I am mulling over the pluses and minuses of those on my list. The joining of norage, rerchy and pepla sounds like a lovely combination of flavors. The tuncooc-oacoc-emlon contains luscious ingredients, ..."

A female interrupted.

"Those are excellent choices, but what about the mur-anaban-recalam dish?"

"And," interjected a third, "the chepa-teanup rettub is scrumptious, or so I am told."

"Why haven't you tried it?" I asked.

"I haven't had the opportunity as of yet. So many choices to consider before finalizing my decision."

We moved through the crowd and approached a couple who actually were tasting some desserts. They were taking quite a while between each spoonful, as they stared off into space as if meditating.

"Are you happy with your choices?" I inquired.

There was a moment that included the appearance of concentrated knitted brows across their large heads as one repeated the word, "happy." He then elaborated.

"I find the term 'happy' to be inexact," he replied. "Now this concoction I am tasting has elements of tartness, sweetness, and a texture of crunchiness. I am trying to calculate the exact amounts of those components that put those elements in balance."

I looked at the cup which held his icy treat.

"It's melting," I pointed out.

"An inescapable example of cause and effect," he said.

I moved toward the counter and squeezed in between those huddled near the casements exhibiting the frozen dessert. I saw one flavor that resembled chocolate chip mint. I pointed to the tub holding the icy treat.

"I'll have some of that," I said, addressing the individual behind the counter.

He seemed to be taken aback by an actual order. He scooped some of the cold mixture into a cup and handed it to me, as the group let out a gasp at the quickness of my choice.

"How can you make such a rash decision without weighing the alternatives, analyzing their ingredients," called out one of the females.

"I like the taste of this flavor," I said, after trying some of the dessert, which was less minty than what I was used to, but still delightful.

"How do you define taste?" the woman asked, her eyebrows raised as if they sought information from a higher source.

"I enjoy the sweetness of the combination," I tried to explain.

She pondered for a few seconds.

"We know that certain substances generate sweetness. But how would we comprehend exactly what constitutes the experience of what is sweet?" she inquired.

I simply said it was an interesting question and the chuckling Definimos and I walked out of the establishment.

"We can get bogged down in our decision-making process. But it is part of who we are. We love to explore all possibilities."

I offered him a taste of the chilled dessert.

"I can sense the aroused effect on my mouth sensors of the one element offset by the pungent ..."

He noticed me staring at him.

"It's very good," he said, and we both smiled.

"Why didn't you have to pay for this?" I asked.

"Ah, a question about economics," he said.

Definimos rubbed his chin and stroked his expansive forehead.

"We started out eons ago with a barter system," he said. "Fine for small agrarian communities. But, let's face it, it's rather difficult to agree on the right trade when all you have are beasts of burden and a few crops and the other person has only eggs from some fowl. We moved on to using what we considered to be precious gems or metals, but that led to some having more than others just based on where they lived, close to rich mines and all, and some acquired this wealth by shall we say unscrupulous means. We then relied on legal tender and eventually on credit tools to charge accumulated funds. After going through all these stages, we found that there were too many deprived of access to worthwhile experiences."

Definimos paused and observed me concentrating on my snack. When he saw I finished, he resumed his discourse.

"We did a great deal of research and conducted numerous discussions with groups that studied financial theories. We decided that each Domandosemprian would receive a certain number of points during each of our time divisions for acquiring housing, food, clothing, and so forth. Purchases would trigger deductions from those point totals. It seemed like an equitable system. However, there were the inevitable squabbles about who should have more points based on what they wanted, what they did for the communities, the number of family members, and so forth, so envy and jealousy still were problems. But then things changed."

"In what way?" I asked.

"I'm glad you asked me that," said Definimos with a beaming smile. "In a word, technology. Our artificial intelligence scientists made amazing breakthroughs. Our automated factories and mobile mechanicals can synthesize just about anything out of the atoms and molecules that comprise existence. No shortages and no pollution. We have all the material things we need, so there is no requirement to pay for anything. We can shed housing like we do clothing, move on to whatever suits us next. However, as time has gone by, our emphasis has been less on material things and more on cerebral pursuits. I would like to say everything is fine, but there have been problems that many of my people do not want to address."

"Like what I just saw at the dessert stand?" I guessed.

Definimos inhaled as if ready to exhale a detailed answer, but then hesitated.

"It seems odd for me to say this," he said. "I think we should hold off any more questions and answers until later. Perhaps you should get some rest before we continue."

Chapter Eighteen

We returned to Definimos's home and he introduced me to his spouse, Pansapianna. She was quite attractive in a large-headed sort of way. She had black hair, and eyes that were more silver than gray, which was a bit unsettling. But then she spoke, and her voice was soothing as it exited a smiling mouth. A mechanical accompanied her.

"This is Auxiliary Mechanical 15268," said Pansapianna. "We have programmed him with a male voice. He provides data and calculations, as he did for me today at my meeting. He helps the children with their schoolwork, and generally aids us in our cerebral inquiries. Samuel, he is at your disposal for the time that you are residing with us. He has a built-in translator to facilitate conversation."

"What do I call him?" I asked.

"You may use a number of salutations," said the mechanical, addressing me. "You may call me by my complete designation, Auxiliary Mechanical 15268. You could just address me by my numerical suffix, which is how the family here calls me."

His voice reminded me somewhat of CP30 from *Star Wars*, quite proper and almost British. I thought for a moment.

"Would it be okay if I just used AM? Besides standing for 'Auxiliary Mechanical,' we use 'AM' as a suffix to designate the time of day in the morning on my planet," I said.

The mechanical turned to Pansapianna.

"Your short preference is not what we are used to," she said. "But I'm sure 15268 can adapt."

"Absolutely," said AM. "Did you wish to call me by that reference because you prefer the daytime on earth?"

"Supposedly we are more alert in the morning, although I am not usually. I could use the help of someone who is," I said. "Also, there was a great thinker from my planet called

Descartes who gave us the saying, 'I think, therefore I am.' Instead of saying 'am,' I will just pronounce the two letters separately."

"Well, even though I am a synthetic, I obviously think, which would justify my existence by that definition," said AM. "My programming allows me to discuss numerous metaphysical and ontological viewpoints, if you so wish."

"I just wanted to use a short version of your name, my chatty friend," I said.

***

The three children joined us for dinner which again entailed numerous choices to be created by what Definimos called the "fabricator," which performed like the "replicators" on *Star Trek*.

I finished eating my meal before my host and his family decided what to have. My food consisted of a bullion-like soup and a sort of soft cheese and vegetable pie which resembled a quiche. The vegetables had the acidic smell and taste of onions but had the consistency of mushrooms. I followed that portion with some fruit that was sweet and had a strawberry texture.

"Do you prefer fowl to livestock on Earth?" asked AM. "Or do all foods have similar tastes on your world?"

I laughed.

"Some do say that everything tastes like chicken, a bird, on Earth," I said. "That's not true, and it's a matter of personal preference what one chooses to eat. Where I come from, we tend to eat heavier meals with various meats as the main course. I noticed so far that is not the custom here."

"Yes, we do not indulge in greasy and fatty substances that would weigh us down," said Pansapianna, as she scrunched her face as if she sniffed something that smelled badly.

"Many individuals on earth are always looking for ways to lose weight, including invasive surgery," I conceded.

"Our culinary technology has provided us with healthy meals that eliminate harmful ingredients, speed digestion and energize metabolism," said Pansapianna. "Besides, we prefer not to become bloated by our food. We find that the overeating of filling courses makes our minds sluggish and hinders cerebral activities."

"I have to admit some of our less healthy foods do taste quite good. Sometimes some of my people do like to reward themselves with some guilty pleasures," I said.

"We encourage indulging in pleasures," said Definimos. "We just want to live long enough to enjoy them."

After dinner, the light food gave way to a plunge into a weighty conversation.

"We were discussing the reasons for believing in a supreme being and an afterlife in school today," said Infinisia, my host's eldest child. "We debated that if there was a deity, why is there so much random chaos in the universe even if there are many examples of order."

"Please provide examples for each side of the argument," said Pansapianna.

"All of the creatures, including us, and plants have intricate, interwoven traits that have perpetuated survival, which would be difficult to write off as having been randomly developed," responded Infinisia. "But, there are terrible diseases --."

"Epidemics," said Hypothico, the visiting boy, next in age.

"Unavoidable accidents," said Thomasina, the youngest.

"Geological upheavals," said Hypothico.

"Environmental threats," said Thomasina, adding to the list.

"We brought these up," said Infinisia. "Even though we have developed scientific means to lessen these threats, there are still lives, even those of children, lost.

"What do you make of this conflicting evidence?" asked Definimos. I liked the Socratic method of questioing.

"There were arguments put forth that said we are undergoing a divine test," said Infinisia. "An omnipotent life form wants to see if we can keep our faith despite hardships. I argued that an infinitely advanced entity should not have such a petty agenda which requires the worship of others."

I admired the insight of this young girl.

"What do you believe and how did you come to your conclusions?" Infinisia asked me.

I pondered her weighty question and then said, "I am a scientist, but I began to have questions about the purpose of existence that neither my mother, a science teacher, nor professors could answer. I felt lost in that place of uncertainty. It was like traveling in a dangerous fog. When my mother passed away when she was so young, I questioned the belief in a benevolent deity, and I never experienced comfort from unsubstantiated religious explanations of reality. Instead, I plunged further into thinking about the scientific mysteries surrounding life and death."

"Do those on your world have these types of discussions?" asked Hypothico.

"Yes, indeed, we have these concerns and debates," I said. "We have various beliefs concerning the existence of a deity, and an afterlife. They have been going on for millennia."

"And what have your people concluded?" asked Infinisia.

I sighed and smiled.

"We're still working on it," I said.

***

Following this discussion, the children left to study more topics, and Pansapianna went to work on her thermodynamics project. A wide screen viewer in the living room area almost filled one wall. Definimos gave me a remote-control device that he programmed to provide translations and subtitles. He urged me to explore the vast menu of transmissions. These consisted of topics ranging from what were the origins of the universe to what were the variables that could predict when a bubble would burst. I asked Definimos if there were any selections that provided pure entertainment.

"Why, these discussions are how we entertain ourselves," he said.

I decided to look at the selection that explored the evolutionary possibilities of Domadosemprians on the planet. The presentation included lengthy discussions from purported experts who contemplated that there would be a time when the body would cease to exist, and an individual would become pure thought. One speaker argued that the body was an obsolete tool for basic survival since mechanicals met that need. Corporeal aspects, he claimed, were limiting and the need to satisfy their wants led to selfish, destructive tendencies.

"Is that possible or even desirable?" I asked Definimos. "What about the way we use the physical senses to gather data for scientific advances? How about the pleasurable sensations that we would lose if the body no longer existed?"

Definimos shrugged.

"Of course, measurements can be accomplished through artificial intelligence, and those enjoyments could be simulated in the brain, which is where they are enjoyed anyway," he said.

"I understand the drive to accumulate more knowledge. But, to what end? On Earth most of the scientific community strives to understand phenomena to better others. What is your purpose? What do you do with your continued search for answers to your questions?"

Definimos thought for a few seconds about this question, which I suppose was exceptionally brief for him.

"Our technology has become so advanced that we do not need to improve our species," he said. "We have eliminated physical needs and have extended our lifespans considerably. Our 'purpose' is to keep exploring topics and searching for answers."

I knew what he was talking about. I was haunted by that part of me that always asked "why?"

"I wish the quest for answers didn't seem never-ending, and so exhausting," I said. "It has provided me little peace."

"I do understand what concerns you," Definimos said. "I will show you soon that we have individuals who suffer from an extreme form of your dilemma. But for my part, I admire your propensity toward questioning. However, your body requires some rest. Maybe someday that will not be necessary, but that is not today."

I acquiesced. I was feeling drained by all the experiences I encountered, and the intellectual wanderings that filled my mind began to exhaust it.

"When is a good time in the morning to start the day," I asked.

"Whenever you think it is right," Definimos answered. "Some want to begin early to get in a full day's worth of inquiries. Others find their mental faculties work best at night."

"We have an expression. It's 'nothing is set in stone.'"

"And a good expression it is!" said Definimos.

Chapter Nineteen

I woke up earlier than the members of my host family. I decided to review entries in my recorded log and added some notes as I recalled extra details about my experiences. The process made me tired even though I had just had a night of sleep. I hungered for some type of physical activity to feed my body's needs and give my mind some waking passive time to digest its thoughts. I went into the spacious living room area and began to exercise, doing running in place, push-ups, and squats.

Infinisia entered the room toward the end of my workout.

"As my mother said, we have dietary and medical means to eliminate the need for excess physical activity, if you wish to take advantage of them," she offered.

"Thank you, but I enjoy exercising," I said. "It gives me some mental relief."

"How does that work?" she asked.

"As I said last night, I have found that I can become agitated when I think too much," I said.

"And your arrival here has generated a great deal of thought, correct?" Infinisia said.

I nodded. She sighed and hesitated before speaking again. "I, too, feel the need to stop thinking about things all the time. It makes me restless, also. How do you deal with this problem, other than exercising?" she asked.

"I was in the military on my home planet," I said. "My experience there taught me that having a daily routine is important. You know, activities that you do each day, like bathing, cooking, cleaning, hobbies. They can become like rituals. In my case, ongoing physical activity can divert my mind."

"We have our tech to take care of many everyday needs," Infinisia said. "Do the rituals, as you call them, help those on your planet?"

"Some more than others," I said.

"It seems that your race lives with conflicting notions," she said.

"You are correct," I said with a smile.

"We learn differently here, "said Infinisia. "Too much of the same way of doing things makes one mired in stagnation."

"I understand that feeling," I said with a sigh. "It would be nice to find a happy medium."

Infinisia thought for a moment and then said, "Can one feel fulfilled in that land of the medium?"

Before I could respond, Definimos entered the room.

"I said I was going to take you somewhere and I would like your input about what is happening at an alarmingly increasing rate here," he said. I could see the concern in his somber attitude and agreed to offer what I could to help.

First, I wished to take a shower after my exercising. Definimos took me to the bathroom so I could wash up. There were buttons in the shower which had icons to press that indicated the water temperature, soap amounts, and the length of the washing and drying. After making my selections, water gushed out from the three sides of the spacious stall. Soap followed, and gentle brushes cleaned me from head to toe. Then I was rinsed and subsequently dried by warm air blowers. Water was sucked out through the drains and even my feet were no longer wet. I dressed and joined Definimos.

"That was a different cleansing experience for me," I said. "I didn't have to do anything."

"I enjoy the time washing," said Definimos. "I stand there with my eyes closed and the automated shower allows me to think about whatever I desire."

Definimos then took me by way of hovercraft to the top section of a building on the outermost edge of Darnounoby. After we entered, he left me in the open atrium for a moment so he could talk with someone sitting behind what looked like a plexiglass desk. The top level of the edifice was divided into many floors which conformed to the inverse pyramid formation. I looked at the lettering above the main desk next to where Definimos now stood, but of course could not decipher it. When Definimos returned to me I asked what the inscription said.

"This place is the Institute for the Mental Perpetuals," he said, as we walked to an escalator. "Housed here are several of us with incredible intellects. But, these individuals have become unstable. We still monitor them for scientific breakthroughs they may discover.

Unlimited virtual reality programs allow them to explore whatever areas of knowledge they wish."

As we ascended to a middle tier floor, I asked Definimos if these individuals permanently lived here. He turned sideways and one eye appeared moist.

"It pains us to limit anyone as to where they may go," he said. "We base our existence on allowing unlimited access to experiences. But those living here are a danger to themselves and others."

We came to one door with writing on it that I assumed was its inhabitant's name.

"This area contains Omnisagarius. He was a pioneer in our use of mechanicals," said Definimos.

We walked through a side door into what turned out to be an observation area. There were monitors around the edges of the seating space which displayed various rooms. Definimos then pushed a button on a side panel. The front wall of the room slid sideways and revealed its occupant sitting behind a transparent barrier in a living room.

"It is a one-way aperture so that we can watch him without his being aware of us," said Definimos.

I watched an elderly, almost emaciated Domandosemprian with an exceptionally large cranium, hooked up to an IV line. A version of a cannula forced what I assumed was oxygen into his nose. Both lines were hooked into the chair on which he sat. He had dark circles around his eyes. He was in the middle of the room staring at realistic holographic projections curving around him. These images consisted of mechanicals and citizens. He spoke as if dictating his thoughts. The translator in my ear allowed me to understand what he was saying.

"Should mechanicals have more arms to aid our citizens?" he asked. "What about more legs to carry out orders more quickly? I wonder if their color matters. Maybe blue is more soothing. But many prefer silver. Would red engender thoughts of violence? Should we construct them to be water compatible to reach areas below ocean surfaces?"

He went on at great length asking questions without slowing down. He started to sound short of breath, but continued to speak. Definimos shut off the speaker.

"He can't make up his mind as to what should be his next project. While trying to decide, he doesn't eat. We had to supplement his nutrition with a feeding apparatus. We inject sleeping solutions so he gets some rest. He hasn't started a project in some time."

"Isn't there a way to provide psychiatric treatment to help him focus his thoughts?" I asked.

Definimos bowed his head and shook it.

"We have tried that way of helping him, but Omnisagarius refuses to let us redirect him into choosing one area of research. When we suggested that he deal with aspects of mechanicals that were more substantive rather than superficial, like their color, he questioned the criteria that differentiated the substantive from the superficial."

"You said some here are a danger to others. Can you show me someone who fits that category?" I asked.

Definimos nodded and we walked to another waiting room. He opened the viewing screen. A naked male was pacing around the edges of his room like a tiger in a zoo cage as he yelled. The chairs in his area were scattered about, with some of their legs broken and their seats ripped apart. Pictures on the walls were askew and slashed. There were broken digital screens thrown about.

"His name is Manarchicredo. He was a philosopher and an author of many treatises," said Definimos. "His writings still are very influential among the populace."

Definimos turned on the speaker and I heard what the man was shouting into a handheld rod which I assumed was recording his words.

"Laws and rules are for those with small minds!" he said. "They are the containers that restrict the natural impulses of the brain to expand, explore, reveal, and understand existence! Throw off your shackles! Push back against all restrictions! All acts are worthy if they further individual freedom and discovery!"

Manarchicredo continued to rant against anything that inhibited the planet's citizens. Definimos switched off the sound emanating from the inner chamber. His face tightened and he had creases lining his visage.

"This was a great man who wrote insightful essays about self-awareness, the sub-conscious mind, and psychological disorders," said Definimos. "However, his eventual extreme stance of indulging the individual will at the expense of any concern for society as a whole found fertile ground in which to grow in our world where we analyze all preconceived beliefs. Some of our people have warped his ideas to justify destruction and the indulgence in taboos, such as incest and violence, instead of restricting questioning to intellectual matters."

Definimos stared at the horizon through one of the room's windows. He seemed in a trance for several moments before speaking again.

"Housed here are the extraordinary among us who have lost their way. But there are many others, as you have seen, who are having trouble functioning every day because they question everything. But, it is not just a practical problem. It is also philosophical. Some see no purpose to existence. They find all belief systems flawed since there are always cavities in them which reveal gaping holes in the logic of those constructs."

We went to another floor in the building which Definimos noted was for those labeled, "Detachers." We did not look directly into the compartments on this level. Instead, we entered a waiting room where Definimos spoke to a few who were present there. We then entered another area which contained several viewing screens. Definimos activated one and I saw a female who paced her room as she spoke to another Domandosemprian.

"The other person is her mental assessor," explained Definimos. He again tapped into the audio feed.

"What seems to be troubling you today?" asked the assessor, another female.

"It's my tongue," the woman said, after which she tugged on the organ for a moment. "I can't stop feeling it attached to me, moving about, rubbing against my teeth! I don't know why I must be tethered to such a strange object!"

Definimos muted the audio and switched on another screen which revealed a male talking to another assessor.

"I am continually aware of my eyes blinking!" He shouted. "All I am drawn to are my eyes opening and shutting, opening and shutting! It's driving me mad!"

Definimos also muted this video.

"We have mind-expanding drugs," he said. "They are marvelous in allowing our people to feel as if they are literally free of the confinements and demands of our bodies. Many of us use them to explore questions we ache to answer. But there are those among us who can't reacclimate to the connection to their corporeal forms after the drugs wear off. Some, as you see here, become psychotically self-conscious about various parts of their bodies. Some have amputated their limbs and ears. That is why we keep them in these horribly restricted places we have padded for their own safety."

We left the building but before I could comment on what I just observed, a loud, deep pulsing sound flooded the area where we walked. The citizens on the skyway where we stood all began to run to the supporting columns.

"It is a Burc attack. It is too dangerous to take the hovercraft," said Definimos, pushing me toward an opening in one of the structures. "We must use the elevators. They contain fortified shielding."

We merged with the rows of Domandosemprians who were funneling into the various lift openings. There was no order as the chaotic, shouting mob pushed and shoved their way to escape. Some fell and were trampled by the crowd whose only unifying aspect was individual survival. The decreased gravity allowed us to move faster than if we were on Burc. We made it inside one of the elevators and it sped downward. I shook out of fear as the bodies of those who hated feeling restricted pressed against me and each other. Many near me cried out as if in pain and banged on the walls of the enclosure.

"They are terrified of confinement," whispered Definimos. "I can hardly tolerate being caged with so many others, even if they are my own people."

I looked through the tall windows of the elevator and saw some spaceships in the sky. They were triangular in shape and reminded me of the Empire's cruisers in the *Star Wars* films. I heard that same deep vibrating sound that emanated on Burc, only here it was part of an offensive and not a defensive maneuver. I then heard distant explosions from where the Burc weapons caused an implosion on the surface. Domandosempria retaliated against the invading crafts by emanating those piercing white beams I had seen coming from their ships as they attacked Burc. We then plunged into darkness until we stopped far below the surface.

When the doors opened, we poured out onto the platform in front of us and the ones in our elevator car ran and merged with others fleeing their lifts toward openings in the underground structure. Definimos led me into one of the cave-like sanctuaries.

"We will be here until we hear an all-clear signal," he said. "The mechanicals also have shelters they automatically retreat to. They will immediately commence repairs once the Burc attack has ceased."

I looked around me and saw cringing looks of fear on some, and wide-eyed, snarling faces on others. I saw similar looks before on those in the battles I participated in on Earth.

"We have endured the sacrifice of this war for generations," said Definimos. "Each side devises more refinements to their weapons to make them more accurate, more deadly. Nobody wins, if there can be any winning with so much suffering. Yet, there are many among us who seem incapable of finding peace with those they see as their mortal enemies."

After hearing Definimos's troubling words I felt now was the time to inform him of my purpose on Domandosempria.

Chapter Twenty

After the Burc attack, we returned to the hovercraft that luckily had not sustained any damage. I decided to trust my host and, after arriving at Definimos's dwelling and finding that we had some privacy, I felt I could speak freely to him.

"I'm afraid I haven't been honest as to how I came to be here," I said. "I did not accidentally arrive on this planet. I invented a propulsion system that can transform matter into waves, travel at the speed of light and then reconvert a ship back to its material form. When in wave mode, I discovered it is also capable of creating a wormhole and that is how I came to be in this part of the galaxy."

Definimos jumped out of his seat, his eyes wide. He began to laugh.

"Why that is marvelous!" he said. "While our mechanicals were repairing your oxygen loss defect, they reported that your craft was unique. Our engineers have been studying it as a matter of course, but they hadn't realized its capabilities. But, why didn't you tell me this sooner ..."

His voice trailed off. His elated expression relaxed into one of contemplation as he again had a faraway look.

"You are afraid it can be a weapon," he said in a monotone. He then began to pace. "I understand your concerns if our scientists learn how to operate it."

"There is a device called a transducer that I hid upon landing. Without it, the ship's propulsion drive will not function," I said. I was quiet and I knew the insightful Definimos realized that if the Seeker was safe, why was I initiating this conversation? I knew he concluded I must have another surprise.

"There's more, then," he said. "No point in holding back anything else."

I took a deep breath before continuing. "My first stop in this sector of space was not here," I said. "It was on Burc."

"How could you not tell me this fact!" Definimos yelled. "Oh, no. I am harboring a Burc spy. My inquisitiveness has put my people in jeopardy!"

But then he quickly quieted down, and he squinted his eyes as he scrutinized me.

"If you are a spy then you would not reveal that you were on Burc," he said. "What is your true purpose here?"

I was relieved that Definimos could think past his passions to reason things out. The tension in my body relaxed after my muscles felt like a boa constrictor trying to crush me.

"There are some people on Burc who feel as you do, that the war between your two worlds must end," I said. "There is one in particular there, a leader, who feels that way, and who protected me. He asked that I come to Domandosempria as an envoy to open a dialogue that might put an end to the hostilities."

I then summarized my experiences on Burc for Definimos. After he seemed to be ruminating on what I had told him, he nodded to himself, as if confirming what he decided.

"There are some on the Governing Brain Trust who would be willing to hear what you have told me," he said. "However, there are several, especially one, Nadatermincos, who will always see the Burcs as a threat to our existence. He has suffered personal loss at the hands of the Burcs, since an attack killed his daughter and grandson. You will have to be careful with him. Also, we discovered that there were numerous historical files onboard your craft. Why did you have those?"

"I wanted to make contact with other worlds and thought we could learn from each other. After my experience on Burc, where inhabitants did not want to risk contamination with exposure to other ways of living, I became cautious about sharing them."

"A noble idea which you followed with a practical choice," said Definimos. "However, I am concerned how Nadatermincos may use the information for his purposes."

Definimos then offered an encouraging smile.

"However, AM, as you call him, has gained access to the files, and hopefully what he finds will allow us to rebut what Nadatermincos argues. If there is a chance at peace, we must try our best to bring it about," he said.

Chapter Twenty-One

Definimos set up a meeting with the Governing Brain Trust. He reminded me that the members were not permanent, and in fact, had no set period of service. The Trust changed often as members came and went.

"The point is," said Definimos, "that whatever the Trust decides today may change tomorrow. Rules here are very flexible."

This unstructured fluctuating form of government irritated me. "That way of running your world is very unstable," I said.

"We see it as resisting rigid rules of behavior," said Definimos.

"Yes, but it allows for confusion and a lack of guidance," I said.

Definimos shrugged.

"It is the price we pay for the extent of our freedom," he said.

Definimos wanted AM to accompany us to supplement any information that we might need at the meeting. As our hovercraft approached the Great Hall where the Governing Brain Trust convened, I became quite anxious. I knew I would feel responsible for many casualties if I failed in this peace initiative. My decision to leave Earth instead of staying and working to end hostilities there made me now feel like a coward. How could I argue for an end to war when I was a deserter from that fight?

As we entered the atrium of the building, I noticed something that startled me. There was a large sheet of shiny silver metal hanging from a staff protruding from the wall. There was a figure etched onto the surface. It was the same capital "U" seated on a straight line that widened into a triangle that I saw at the entrance to The Safe on Burc.

AM became aware of my observation of the interior of the edifice. "Notice the soaring walls here and the pointed ceiling," said AM. "It symbolizes the desire to reach the pinnacle of learning on Domandosempria."

"I need something more specific ..." I began to say before AM interrupted me.

"I am fully versed in all aspects of the minute details of this edifice. For instance, I can relate when the building's foundation began ...

"What is the specific meaning of that hanging symbol?" I asked, the words shooting out of my mouth as quickly as bullets before AM could go off on another tangent. I swiftly thought that at least the Burcs knew when to keep quiet.

"As I said before, I do like your inquisitive mind," commented the smiling Definimos. "And your question is one we have been asking ourselves for some time. We found it almost hidden among the excavated dwellings of some of our ancestors."

"It was even sewn into the lining of clothing and etched on some jewelry," added AM.

"Yes," said Definimos. "We have determined that our people did not originate on this planet since we have not found evolutionary evidence supporting that theory. Long ago, our archaeologists discovered the remains of a spacecraft, and historical records relate stories of the arrival of the first of our race. However, if there were any records of their origins we did not find them. We would be very grateful if we could someday make sense of this mystery surrounding our beginnings. In the meantime, it has become a symbol for us to continue our quest to understand all things. It looks like a bird that can fly above any attempt to cage it."

I felt my heart quicken as Definimos spoke. I hoped that what I was about to tell him would not alienate him from me. I was counting on his inquisitiveness to scale the mountain of prejudice that rose over years of animosity.

"When I was on Burc," I said, "I saw that exact same symbol. It was on a type of fortress which the Burcs call The Safe which may contain secrets about the origins of the Burc people."

Definimos stepped back several feet as if to eye me from a wider perspective. His piercing, unblinking look made me feel like he was trying to see through my words to my very being.

"Is this some type of ploy?" he asked. "Perhaps your purpose here is to confuse and delay us so that Burc will be able to attack while we are preoccupied assessing the meaning of this claim you have made."

"I assure you that is not the case," I said.

"But you bring no proof, no evidence whatsoever of this outlandish claim. Perhaps Burcs spied on us and stole the symbol to deceive us and manipulate you."

"The engraving I saw was very old," I said. "The Burc I told you about, Lask, was a sincere being. He said that he also did not know what the symbol meant. I believed him. And now you must believe me. There is a link between your two cultures."

"It is an interesting hypothesis, worthy of further exploration, which is at the heart of Domandosemprian beliefs," commented AM.

Definimos began to pace and was quiet for a while. When he stopped moving he stared at me as he nodded his head.

"Very well," he said. "You should present your case to the Trust. If what you have told me is true, I hope that we can move the Trust's members to explore the ramifications of this discovery, and possibly move closer to a peaceful resolution with Burc."

We entered the room where the Governing Brain Trust met. It was expansive with many mirrors which reflected images off into infinity. It was noteworthy for having a roof which, as the Domandosemprian members entered, began to retract, opening the inside space to the outside, and merging the two. I felt dwarfed by the layout of the chamber and intimidated as to my ability to carve out a portion of the space with my diminutive presence.

The members sat down at a large table that was in the form of an elongated figure eight, like the shape of a Domandosemprian spacecraft. Definimos led me to a seat at the narrow center of the table. Once there, one of those present began to speak.

"My name is Perpetuamenta," she said. "Definimos has told us of your amazing journey to our sector of the universe. Quite impressive. He originally informed us of your account of leaving your own planet and accidentally stumbling upon a wormhole that brought you here."

She hesitated for a moment, leaned toward me, and opened her eyes widely as if inspecting something exceedingly small. I felt uncomfortable and started to smell the damp odor of my own sweat.

"However, he has now provided information that you invented the propulsion system that brought you here and that you did not just happen upon a wormhole. He also has told us that you were on the planet Burc before arriving on Domandosempria and are on an important mission."

Perpetuamenta stopped again, retracted her microscopic gaze, and sat back in her chair before speaking again.

"So, what is the message you bring to us from our enemies on Burc?"

I felt that was a loaded question and put me at the disadvantage of trying to argue for a truce with Burc. But I persevered.

"I am here to tell you that not everyone on Burc is your enemy," I said. "There is at least one of their rulers, a Proc, named Lask, who seeks peace after so much fighting. He asked me to be a neutral emissary to suggest a meeting between the leaders on Domandosempria and the ones on Burc who feel that the war between your two worlds has lasted long enough."

"How do we know that this action isn't some sort of tactic to undermine our security."

It was Nadatermincos who spoke, the one that Definimos warned me about. He was older than the others there, with a wrinkled face and sparse gray hair. His nose appeared pinched, as if he was smelling spoiled fruit.

"Our ancestors tried to deal with the Burcs a long time ago," he continued. "We attempted to enlighten them as to their repressive ways. And what thanks did we receive? They attacked us and drove us off their planet after we landed there to reach out a helping hand."

"That was then, and this is now," I countered. "There has been a great deal of blood that has spilled over time. As long as neither world tries to impose its will on the other, hostilities could cease."

"It is the Burc nature to force its will on others," said Nadatermincos. He reached out his arms and tightened his fists. "They are incapable of dealing with the existence of anyone who questions their rigid rules."

"There are now some who want peace more than justification for their way of life," I said.

I hesitated before continuing. I wasn't sure, after Definimos's initial reaction, if I should state what I saw on Burc and now on Domandosempria about the importance of the "U" symbol. I decided to gamble.

"I noticed the large 'U' seated upon a triangle outside this hall. Definimos told me it is a mysterious relic rooted in your past that has come to mean the desire to seek knowledge. The Burcs base much of their designs on the triangle. At an archeological site on Burc I saw the same symbol that adorns this Great Hall. Surely there must be a connection between your two worlds worth exploring."

There was a general uproar of voices from the members present, a chaotic mingling of individuals all speaking at the same time. Definimos looked at me and then shouted above the others in an attempt to come to my rescue.

"We have long sought the answer to questions about the symbol. We now have an opportunity to discover more concerning it. Isn't that what we Domandosemprians do? We question, investigate, search, analyze, hypothesize. Here is an opportunity to fulfill our purpose and end the fighting, too. Why not take advantage of the situation?"

"Because it may be a trap to lower our defenses and become the victims of a surprise attack as we indulge our inquisitiveness," yelled Nadatermincos.

"I know about the cost of war," I said as I interrupted the two. "I was a soldier on my planet, Earth. I have sought to escape the ravages of violence and I hope all of you will, too."

Nadatermincos left his seat and approached me. But, it was to the others that he directed his remarks.

"Why should we accept the words of this limited creature to sway us?" he said, pointing to me. "How can we give weight to his requests? I would like to ask him several questions to gauge how seriously we should consider what an individual from his planet has to say."

Numerous members called out their agreement to the action proposed by Nadatermincos. I adjusted my earbud to ensure I heard the translation clearly.

"We now know something of your planet's history based on your ship's computer files," said Nadatermincos. "What we have ascertained does not paint a particularly praiseworthy portrait."

Nadatermincos turned to the Trust and used his right hand to jab at points for emphasis, as if stabbing at an opponent.

"It seems on this man's planet there was a people known as the Egyptians who ruled for centuries based on their rigid societal and religious beliefs. They felt that they were superior to a race called the Jewish people, who the Egyptians used as slaves to build monuments to their own hubris. Am I correct?"

"Yes," I said, trying to regroup, "but what followed …"

"What followed," said Nadatermincos, "was war upon war throughout time as one individual or group of people tried to conquer another and impose its way of living on its subjects: Alexander the Great (was he really deserving of such a title?); the Roman emperors; the various Islamic regimes; the Catholics with their crusades and barbaric Inquisition, which burned people for questioning accepted ways of thinking. And as time marched on, various armies imposed their power over others. The Nazis were the best at squashing any deviations from their lies about them being the superior race."

"However," inserted AM., "the records show that there have been numerous instances of generosity, charity, and evolutionary advances during Earth's history …"

"Yes, we have evolved in many respects," I said, trying to restore balance to the accusations, although I felt overwhelmed by the evidence of barbarity in my planet's history. "My country, the United States, devised a democratic system with laws that can allow for change and justice."

Nadatermincos turned back to me. As he approached, he thrust the fingers of his left hand at my chest, and I felt like a person without a foil in a duel.

"Yes," he said, "Let's talk about your country. Your ancestors wrote about the importance of freedom while enslaving others just because they came from somewhere else, and looked different, and thus considered them inferior by those unevolved criteria. Many of your countrymen continue to adhere to those prejudicial, hateful beliefs to this day. There have been laws and practices to suppress the unfortunate in your society and prevent them from participating in your precious democracy."

"But there have been great people," I said, "Who have fought for justice and freedom …"

"Many of whose attempts have been overturned and some of those persons have been assassinated," said Nadatermincos. "Admit it. Your country looks good in theory. In practice, a small number of rich and powerful people impose their will on the unempowered. They feed them lies that they frame as absolute truths so that their underlings will comply with the rulers' wishes. In short, the inhabitants of Earth consist of a predominantly unenlightened, bigoted population."

I became flustered and was about to protest but found it difficult to summon the words. Before I could say anything, Nadatermincos spoke again.

"Our examination of your spacecraft indicates that there is a piece of machinery that is missing that would allow the propulsion system to work. I would like to suggest to this august body that Galloper knows where this instrument is located. When it is restored we can investigate how to use it against our enemy."

I looked at Definimos who then addressed the Trust.

"I would like a few moments to confer with our guest," he said, and after he received approval of his request he took me aside.

"I am sorry for how this meeting is proceeding," he said in a hushed voice to me. "I may be able to get a recess and appeal to other members who are more sympathetic to not pursuing the use of new weapons."

Nadatermincos's words hit me like a hand slapping me out of a dream state. What he said was all too true. My people were vile in many ways, repressive and inflexible.

"He's right," I said, feeling defeated. "Why should they listen to one of my kind. Burc embodies so many of the worst aspects of the people of my planet. Perhaps your world should use all means necessary to protect your own species and keep its citizens free."

"I know that the Burcs are a totalitarian threat. But, we agreed," argued Definimos, "that war just begets more war. It has spawned generations of casualties. Help me take a stand here."

As my head began to throb from the conflicting pressures exerted upon it, the alarm sounded again. The Burcs were back.

Chapter Twenty-Two

The Trust started to evacuate the chamber and Definimos ushered me behind AM as we entered the hallway.

"We must not allow the Trust to use your invention," said Definimos as we rushed to the hovercraft. "Nobody should turn it into a weapon. Its original purpose was to be a tool for acquiring knowledge, and we must fight to keep it that way."

There was that dreaded deep vibrating sound from above as a Burc spaceship targeted a building close to where we ran. I heard the loud groaning sound of a structure collapsing. The ground forces emitted the brilliant white light beams into the sky to counter the attack. We reached our hovercraft, and Definimos gave AM the order to return to his home. AM piloted the vehicle with precision to avoid the Burc bombardment. Definimos used a slender, inverted pyramid-shaped communication device to contact Pansapianna.

"My family is in the shelter below our building," said Definimos, after speaking to his spouse. "I believe the two of us must use your spacecraft to go to Burc and explore this Safe to determine whatever connection there may be between our two planets. I see this plan as our best option to stop this war."

I shook my head.

"The Burcs are very resistant to any possibility of finding out facts that may change their way of life," I said. "They are not going to allow a Domandosemprian on their planet, let alone one to enter one of its restricted sites."

"You said your benefactor there sent you to start a peace initiative," said Definimos. "We can use him to secure our secret mission."

"I think it's hopeless," I said, feeling unworthy of such a task. It seemed as if I was helplessly falling down the deep chasm that divided these two entrenched cultures.

Definimos shook me, as if attempting to awaken my sense of purpose.

"We must try to overcome your negativity," he urged.

We arrived at Definimos's building. AM and I stayed in the hovercraft as Definimos went to talk to his wife and children. He returned with more earbuds and a piece of equipment that was in the shape of a circular disc with a clip attached to its back.

"I needed a portable translating hub to facilitate communication with your Burc ally," said Definimos. "What is his name again?"

"Lask," I said. "I hope you two will get along, but I have my doubts."

"We both seek peace," said Definimos. "Beyond that desire, I'm not sure we are at all compatible. Here, put this clothing on and raise the hood over your head to disguise yourself."

Definimos told AM to fly the hovercraft to an area outside of Darnounoby. We approached what looked like an airfield and several of the Domandosemprian figure-eight-shaped spaceships were there. Just seeing them again caused me to tremble when I remembered the attacks on Burc.

"You must remain inaudible," said Definimos. "Your Seeker is at this location for investigation. I will attempt to convince the workers here that the Trust has authorized me along with a mechanical and a security expert, the role you will play, to inspect your spacecraft to make sure there is protection from any Burc attacks. We can then fly to where you hid the transducer and then go to Burc."

We exited the hovercraft, and several individuals approached us as we made our way toward one of the hangers. I pulled my hood down far enough over my face to avoid detection. I stood several yards behind Definimos and the others. I leaned forward but could not hear what they were saying. AM turned toward me.

"You are endeavoring to audit the conversation," AM said. "I will attempt to help you. Despite Definimos being a member of the Governing Brain Trust, he is not able to issue any commands. He must logically argue that the Trust is in lockdown at the moment but sent us to determine the Seeker's status so that Burc forces do not discover it. These discussions can last for a while since numerous questions are posed. To pass the time, would you like a historical lecture on the geological aspects of this area?"

I declined what I was sure AM's gripping discourse and preferred to contemplate how to facilitate the meeting between two adversaries by stressing that they had arrived at the same conclusion although coming from different perspectives. I hoped we could get to the Seeker soon, since when the Burc attack ceased the Trust would discover our activities.

After an extended conversation, Definimos stopped speaking and returned to us.

"I have convinced them of the merits of my argument," he said. "Follow me and say nothing."

One of the Domandosemprians with whom Definimos was talking led us into a hanger, which had openings at both ends to facilitate entrance and exit of aircraft. I was thrilled to see the Seeker there. I felt a sense of paternal relief reuniting with my technological offspring. The exterior hatch was open and we entered the main cabin. Definimos whispered something to AM who proceeded to administer what looked like the Vulcan nerve pinch employed by Spock on *Star Trek* to incapacitate our escort. The worker passed out and AM deposited the unconscious fellow outside the Seeker.

I closed the hatch on the spacecraft, input my security codes, switched on the craft's systems, and quickly checked to ensure that everything was working properly, including the oxygen level. Satisfied, I sat in the pilot's chair. AM used his android strength to secure himself by holding onto metal supports. Definimos strapped himself into the hammock. I powered up the cruising drive which was meant for transport on planet surfaces. I synced my watch's GPS coordinates for the transducer to the onboard locator system. I initiated the ignition sequence. The Seeker's collision sensors avoided the hanger's walls and roof, and the craft soared out of the building. We headed to the location where I first landed on the planet. After a smooth touchdown, I left the ship and used my watch to lead me to where I concealed the transducer. I retrieved it and once inside the Seeker I reinstalled the device.

I accessed the onboard computer's memory and punched in the location of Burc as the destination. I needed to inform Definimos of the HOPS effect.

"The two times that I used the harmonic drive, I experienced strange visions. I'm not sure as to what causes this effect. It may have something to do with converting matter into wave mode. Perhaps transforming the body into an energy state releases any confines on one's individual consciousness and connects it to a time continuum. It's sort of scary."

"Not really. That sounds absolutely exhilarating!" said the awed Definimos. "I look forward to the experience."

I smiled and shook my head, realizing how different were our ideas of danger and excitement. But, I was encouraged by Definimos's exuberance. Before I engaged the HOPS, AM said, "Samuel, does your propulsion drive work the same on synthetic life forms as it does on organic ones? I was just wondering, will my neural processing system revert to its previous form upon reconversion? I would prefer that it would, since I might not recognize myself if it did not, and I am not sure if I am programmed to adapt to that disorienting experience."

"It seems you are having a mechanical version of fear, AM," I said. "I wish I could calm your digital distress. But, I do not know what will happen to you. I hope you will remain intact."

"I have no experience in functioning on hope," AM said.

"Well, in that way you're not much different from many people I knew. But, let's give it a try," I said, and I initiated our journey.

Part Three

The Safe

Chapter Twenty-Three

During the conversion to the wave state my vision became clouded, as if I was in one of those movies where they used dry ice to create a thick mist. Images seemed to suddenly appear and then disappear. I saw beings that looked human at one point, and then transformed into Burcs the next second, and subsequently took on Domandosemprian features. The visions ended with the appearance of bright light that then faded to reveal a view of Earth from space. Then everything dissolved into blackness. The darkness slowly dissipated, and I saw the cabin of the Seeker, as if I had just awakened from a dream. I let out a sigh, relieved that the HOPS returned us to the matter state.

I looked at Definimos as he opened his eyes and a smile began to stretch across his mouth.

"Quite exhilarating," he said. "I saw various landscapes, fertile and barren ones. I could see very far away but also objects close to me were magnified. There were discordant sounds, quite harsh, but they were offset by beautiful music with voices singing in harmony. Fascinating."

I shared my HOPS vision. We then both looked at AM who then stared at us for a moment.

"Oh, I see," he said. "It is my turn. I did not see what either of you reported. There were individual, separate clips of images. I witnessed a physical joining of a couple of organic beings. They looked like Domdandosemprians, but their forms kept changing in shape. Then there was the birth of a child. I also witnessed the death of those same shape-shifting beings. It wasn't so much what I saw, but that I had associated reactions to what I viewed that was surprising. It was more like waves of electrical impulses flooding my sensors. It was not quantifiable."

"It sounds like you were experiencing emotions," I said.

"I do not understand how that could occur," said AM "However, I also recorded data as to the number of pixels illuminated, the decibels of sound, the speed of the craft, and more if you would like me to inform ..."

"Maybe later," I said, cutting off our informative friend. "Right now, we can see Burc on the viewer."

I programmed the Seeker to land a walkable distance to the site of The Safe, but also behind a jagged outcropping of rock to hide its location. I retrieved the communications wand that Lask gave me before I left for Domandosempria. I pressed the button on its side and heard a series of three beeps followed by a short pause. I then heard Lask's voice.

"Yes," he said.

"It's Sam. I am back," I said in Burc.

"I am glad to hear your voice," Lask said in a hushed response, but which could not hide excitement in his voice. "It has been some time. Have you brought good news?"

"I have brought more than that," I said. "Are you safe?"

"Yes, the Procs think you flew off the way I told them," Lask said. "I am on my way to my hut."

"You must meet me at The Safe," I said. "Come with food and drink. When you get there, turn off the bots at the cave."

Chapter Twenty-Four

I again detached the transducer and hid it a safe distance from the Seeker. We approached the site where The Safe extended below the surface of the ground. I told AM and Definimos to be quiet and stay hidden behind a boulder until Lask arrived. We didn't have to wait long before he appeared. He rode in a tram and as a couple of bots approached his vehicle, he exited it and pulled out a wand. He activated the instrument and the bots became still. I motioned to Definimos and AM to follow me. Lask saw us approach and as we drew closer, he became agitated, turning around and stomping a foot.

"What have you done!" he yelled. "I sent you to make peace, not to bring one of them back here! He will cause the Procs and the rest of the Burcs to say you turned on us and I helped our foe. They will think there is a new plot for his world to make us slaves!"

When Definimos heard Lask's translated words he became angry. I had already set the translator to generate the Burc language. I handed an ear bud to Lask so he could understand what the Domandosemprian was saying, although that was probably not a good idea.

"I have put myself in danger with my own people," said Definimos, "and subjected my body and mind to a technology that transformed my atoms, I risked all to see if we could find some common ground. I did not make these sacrifices for a tiny-minded ingrate to insult me!"

Lask addressed me, ignoring Definimos.

"Are you sure he is not a spy?" he asked. "Is he here to find out how to beat us? His kind came here once to make us live as they do. We look to end the war, but not if it means we lose who we are. I can't be a part of a plan that will harm my world!"

Lask turned and headed back to the tram. I ran after him and grabbed his arm. I spoke to him in English and relied on the translator.

"We are trying to save your world from war," I said. "I come from a place that has been almost destroying itself for millennia. It never seems to end, and it makes me ill to see the same thing happening here."

"I do not know of your home," said Lask. "But I do know his kind. He has fooled you so he can come here to snake his thoughts into our minds to make the Burcs fight each other."

I was feeling defeated again, having left Earth because I couldn't change things for the better there, and now failing again here. But, somehow I couldn't just surrender to hatred and bigotry that led one group of people to view another race as a sworn enemy.

"Definimos was my host on Domandosempria," I said. "He protected me, informed me of the planet's activities, and seeks an end to the fighting just as much as you do. He prevented his people from using my invention as a weapon against the Burc." I switched to the Burc language to add impact to my words. "You know I do not lie to you, so trust me now when I say that he is here to help."

Lask was quiet, and although he shook his head, as if dismissing what I said, he also darted glances at me and Definimos, as if trying to let in what I said to him. Since I knew contemplation of various choices was practically painful to a Burc, I played my wild card.

"Lask, the drawing on The Safe," I said for the translator. "The one that looks like a bird with curved wings that sits on a line and ends in a triangle? I saw the same image on the building where the Domandosemprian leaders meet."

Lask's eyes widened, which almost made his head look larger.

"It can't be," he said in an almost inaudible voice.

"It is true," said AM. "My memory files validate the authenticity of the depiction on Domandosempria."

"We believe our ancestors brought the figure to us," said Definimos. "I would very much like to see the one on this planet."

Lask paced about, mumbling to himself. Sometimes his voice became alternately louder and quieter as he shifted the direction of his walking and turned his head from side to side. At one point he banged one hand against the side of his leg as if in anger. It looked to me like he was arguing with himself. He then glanced at us only for a moment, lowered his gaze, and then nodded his head in agreement. I gave out a loud sigh of relief and we started to walk down the embankment on the carved-out stairs to the flat landing at the bottom. We passed through the arched entrance into the cave with carvings.

"Definimos," I said, "from what we can tell from this ancient writing it says here 'the way to joy is through peace that comes when one joins with the foe.' There is also an invitation to enter, and 'learn of the past.'"

"The translator hub I have brought can scan written languages and convert them into known tongues," said Definimos. "Let's see if your assessment of the words is accurate."

After he aimed a beam of light that emanated from the translator, Definimos read the interpretation in Domandosemprian.

"Fascinating," said Definimos. "There are a couple of words that are different: 'path' instead of 'way;' 'happiness' instead of 'joy;' 'enemy' instead of 'foe;' ..."

"Yes, yes," said an impatient Lask. "These are small things."

"In any event," said Definimos with a sideways squint at Lask, "that etching is obviously an expression advocating the positive nature of unifying with an opponent."

"Must you use such large words to say what is plain," complained Lask, since he could hear the length of Definimos's statement even before the translation reached his ears.

"The right expressions are necessary to understand the nuances of what is said. It's better than the grunts you produce," said Definimos.

"There is an expression on Earth," I said, trying to end the discord. "It says, 'You go to your church, I'll go to mine.'"

"An interesting metaphorical comment on tolerance," said Definimos.

"At least it is short and to the point," said Lask as he turned away as if to prevent further discussion.

Lask had brought bags of food and canisters of water. We approached the large door, and Lask explained how it was easy to enter. Burcs who did so and returned unsuccessfully said they found themselves in the dark, as if awakening from a deep sleep. Spotlights, triggered by their motion, led them back to the entrance. They exited through the same portal with their memories of the past year erased.

"It is obviously a test," said Definimos. "And those who attempted to take the examination failed, having returned with no knowledge to help future Burcs who sought to discover facts about the planet's history inside. I say we join forces and see if the information within can help us to attain a peaceful solution to our dilemma."

After a moment of contemplation, we looked at each other and nodded our various-sized heads in agreement. We approached the door, and I pushed the button on the right side to open it at the same time that Lask reached out in a failed attempt to stop me. A blue light fanned out from above the portal and appeared to scan us. The door did not open.

"The bot may not go through," said Lask. "We tried with one of ours and the door stayed closed. When we sent it off, then the Proc could go in."

"It's possible that the test requires individuals to solve problems without any outside technological help," I said.

"Well AM," said Definimos, "it looks as if this place is anti-mechanicals. Please return to the spacecraft and maintain surveillance there."

"Very well," said AM. "But, I would have found it stimulating to explore this structure, and add the information to my programming so as to analyze and disseminate my findings."

As AM walked away, Lask looked at Definimos and commented, "I'm glad he's gone. He has as big a mouth as you."

I pushed the button which again initiated the scanning beacon. This time the wide metal door slowly slid to the right, allowing the three of us access to the interior. Once inside the door closed behind us, and the room was dark for a moment. Suddenly, lights turned on and we found that we were in a circle of illumination created by a huge spotlight. I approached the door through which we entered and found it smooth with no handle and no button on the inside. I tried to slide it, but I could not budge it.

We walked forward and the spotlight followed our movement. There was an archway before us. We passed through it into another chamber. The spotlight disappeared and then brilliant lights vanquished the temporary darkness, revealing a large domed room. In front of us was a raised platform lit by green light which had three steps to access it. We ascended the area which looked like a stage. Then holographic images appeared in the center of the area. Animations of two humanoids appeared, which had rudimentary outlines of heads, arms, hands, and trunks, along with legs and feet. Their head size approached more the shape of humans on Earth than inhabitants on either Burc or Domandosempria. Both Lask and Definimos looked at me when they saw the figures, and I shrugged, not being able to explain what we were watching. I knew nobody from my planet had the technology in the past to travel here. The figures were blue in color. In front of the holograms two vertical lines appeared together followed by a space and then two more lines. The animated figures then drew four lines. An opening appeared to the right and the figures moved through it. The scene was repeated, but this time the figures drew three lines. A beam with the sharpness of a laser shone from the ceiling, split in two and hit the heads of the two figures. The blue disappeared and the heads turned colorless. An opening appeared to the left and the abstractions walked through it.

"It looks like their brains were wiped," said Lask, "just as those Procs who came back to us."

"Yes," agreed Definimos. "We have just witnessed an example of how to play the game. The Safe will present a problem. If we answer correctly, we get to move forward. If not, the beams will erase our memories, and our journey terminates. Quite ingenious!"

"Back on Earth," I said, "there were these places many years ago that would allow people to solve problems together. We called them escape rooms. In order to continue playing the game you had to solve each room's puzzle until you could exit the structure."

"It sounds quite amusing," offered Definimos.

"The only thing that happened if you failed was that they let you leave," I said. "There was no wiping of recent memories."

"Burcs are trained to play these types of games," said Lask. "I can help here."

Lask's optimistic attitude encouraged me, but that feeling quickly vanished after we saw what followed. There was a projection of a white room with a small bed in the center that resembled a bassinet. Four adults and two children stood on either side of it, wearing clothes of varying colors and designs.

The figures appeared to be male and female by the shapes of their bodies. There was another female adult who had on a light-colored coat and held instruments in her hands which she appeared to use to examine what was inside the bassinet. She then reached down and picked up a motionless baby. She looked at the others in the room and shook her head. The others, which I assumed were family members, began to cry and a couple of the adults fell to the ground and screamed as if in agony. The medical person tried to hand the child to one of the kneeling females. She covered her face with her hands, and shook her head. I assumed it was the mother who could not accept that her baby was dead.

The scene went dark for a moment and then the lights came back on. That projection ended and another took its place which presented a congregation of individuals in a large circular room with a high ceiling. There was a tiny carved box that was situated on a platform in the center of the area. There was a male close to it with flowing, gold robes who then circled the raised spot moving his hands as if performing a blessing. The occupants cried and sobbed. The lights once more were extinguished. Then there appeared a three-dimensional rendering of a stark white living area with windows and two chairs situated far apart on which sat a female and a male from the first scene. They looked down and there was no communication between the two. The following scene presented the disturbing image of the inert body of the man in a sunken tub. Red liquid, which I assumed simulated blood, flowed into and mixed with water in which he was immersed. The woman then walked into the room and raised her hands to her face in horror, and gave out a shriek.

The projections ceased and lights illuminated the room in which we stood. A divided screen presented various pictorial images that seemed like a movie storyboard. There was a tutorial which showed a figure moving the images around as if to place them into a sequence, adding some from the second section of the screen and discarding other images into a disposal icon. There was also a creator tool to make new images. There was a clock high up on the wall behind the stage. The face was green and it had a black hand that began to move clockwise. As it did so, the green background behind the hand turned white.

"What are we to do here?" Lask asked, his words scrunched together as if trying to save time.

"We have the traumatic death of an infant which has led to another tragedy," said Definimos. "I believe we are to visualize the nature of existence and its ramifications."

"That is no help!" yelled Lask. "There is no point to that, and we will not move on."

"Well then, how are we to help those who suffer tragedy unless they have a broader construct in which to determine the meaning of their lives in the universe?" asked Definimos.

"I don't know what you just said," said Lask, shaking his head. "Those who lose a child need to do things, not think of them. That will make them feel worse!"

"Pretending there is nothing wrong just delays the impact of the premature loss of children." countered Definimos. "I suggest first questioning the idea of the belief in a divine entity that would allow such grief to be visited upon a child and family. Of course, we must take into consideration the concept of not knowing the larger plan of the universe. What do you think, Samuel?"

I was experiencing a sense of doom, looking at the expanding white on the clock face. It felt as if the timer was on an explosive device which was counting down to a detonation.

"I think we better hurry up with a plan if we like our brains the way they are," I said.

"How each fits in with the whole is what all want," said Lask, trying to apply himself to the task. "To have that, each one must know his or her place in the scheme of things.

Death is part of that scheme. The whole web of life is what counts, not each thread. The loss of one piece makes way for the next."

"Very good argument," said Defnimos. "I am impressed with the poetic expression of your viewpoint. But it only addresses half of the problem. We may be part of the whole, but we are still individuals with personal desires and feelings. There should be no suppression of those aspects of sentient beings, or else we become something less than what we are."

"Fellas," I said as I started to sweat. "You two must work together. That is the only way we get the answers that this place contains." I paused, thinking about how I could guide them further. "This problem does not contain a simple mathematical solution. I think offering a path of positive action is the key here."

Definimos and Lask both nodded their heads at the same time and approached the interactive screens. They spoke to each other as they moved images around, discarded some possibilities, and developed new ones. Definimos constructed a scenario that provided individual counseling to the couple that lost their child, and support groups that consisted of others that underwent similar trauma. The groups' leaders acted out question and response sessions that mirrored occurrences surrounding upsetting experiences, such as accidents, suicides and diseases. Lask used his Burc puzzle-solving skills, and his contribution included using groups of families, neighbors, and friends gathering to support the grieving couple and diverting them with housekeeping, and outings. Lask also set up a listing of community and personal activities in which the bereaved parents could engage to keep them active. Lask and Definimos stopped for quick breaks to drink some water and wipe the sweat from their respective sized brows.

After the two worked on the problem for several hours, the simulation shut off after they were finished and there was a gap of a minute with no additional inputs on the part of Definimos and Lask. Three chimes sounded and the room became dark. I felt my pulse quicken. Were we about to become additional entries on the list of failures that preceded us, forced to return outside to our inexorable fates? Then, a white spotlight lit a part of one of the walls to the right side of the stage. A door slid open, and we knew that Lask and Definimos were successful. We smiled at each other and headed for the opening.

"We may be blessed to see what the Gens have hid from us all these years!" said Lask in a voice sounding more excited than any I heard since I knew him.

After we crossed the threshold into the next chamber, the door slid closed behind us. I observed that there was no way to retrace our steps just as before. The entrance area slanted so that we were descending downward. The room, which was dark, brightened, and again we found ourselves in another large domed space. In front of us was a raised platform that copied the preceding one, lit by green light and with three steps in front of it. There was the clock with the green face that seemed to dare us to look at it.

"Oh no!" said Lask as he closed his eyes and shook his head. "Why are we not done? Must I work with this man once more?"

"I share your displeasure," said Definimos, almost spitting out the words. "Only raise it to the tenth exponential degree."

I let out a loud sigh. "Now boys," I said, hoping to keep my companions focused. "You two are still at the grumbling stage, and the process to have you both working together will take some time. It seems our hosts knew that would be the case. You didn't really think reaching our goal would be that quick, did you?"

"What is 'quick' is not the same for you and me," said Lask, shaking his head and walking away.

Chapter Twenty-Five

There was no new holographic display as we mounted the platform in the second chamber. Instead, the clock on the wall started counting down with only half of its surface colored green. A side door opened. I passed through the opening and found what looked like a restroom, with an oval seat situated over an open tank of liquid and a button attached to the tank. I pushed the button and an antiseptic-smelling liquid flushed into the receptacle, which then drained. There was a dispenser on the wall with a switch next to it. I turned it clockwise and a gel dripped out. From the pungent smell I deduced it was an alcohol-based sanitizer. There was a button next to the entrance to the room. When I pushed it the door slid closed and then opened on the second push. I showed my companions the room.

"From what you have said, Samuel, this edifice is ancient. It is admirable that the conditions here have been maintained so well after centuries. Our absent hosts were quite considerate," said Definimos. "Excuse me while I make use of the hygienic accommodations."

After he closed the door, Lask shook his head.

"So much to say for just dropping waste," he said.

I stared at him.

"What is wrong?" he asked.

"You just said 'dropping.' Two sounds at once," I said.

"Hm," uttered Lask. He then just waved his hand as if dismissing the observation.

After we all used the facilities, Definimos began to open one of the bags that contained a grainy bread loaf that I had previously eaten on Burc, and the sweet water that Lask offered me on my first day on his planet. Lask grabbed the bag from Definimos.

"Why do you do this?" he said. "You will waste food!"

Definimos sighed and rolled his eyes.

"Don't you see that we have been given the opportunity to rest, relieve ourselves, and partake of sustenance?" he said. "That is why there hasn't been any new challenge yet and the timer is set for a shortened period."

I turned to Lask.

"He is right," I said. "We should use this time to get our strength back."

Lask paused for a moment and then nodded his head. We sat down on the floor facing each other.

"You did quite well in the last room," said Definimos to Lask.

I smiled, realizing the Domandoemprian used monosyllabic words.

"Thank you. You too," said Lask, as he handed Definimos some of the bread and liquid.

After eating we stretched out on the floor and fell asleep. I dreamed of walking on the beach at Ocean City, New Jersey when I was young. My family lived in a suburb of Philadelphia for a time, which was only about a ninety-minute drive away from the shore resort. I liked the feeling of strolling for miles as the distant, yet comforting, sun wrapped its warmth around me, and the expansive ocean reached out to touch my feet on its border. Three loud gong sounds woke me up, pulling me out of that feeling of equilibrium.

The clock's face was all white now. We packed up our supplies and we knew it was time to proceed. We walked up the steps to the platform which triggered the next holographic display.

Three dimensional projections depicted a planet where exhaust smoke from buildings, passenger vehicles, and tools darkened the sky. There were trash-filled waterways. The oceans began to rise and inundate shore areas. Creatures resembling fish, birds, and reptiles, disappeared in multiple flashes of light. The vast landscape of the simulated planet became devoid of life. The sound of howling winds accompanied the projected images. There was then the depiction of a blizzard snowfall, as the temperature dropped in the room, and we shared frigid air for a few minutes. The simulation shut down and in its place were graphics representing the landscape we just viewed and a tutorial on how it could be manipulated through touchscreens. The clock again had a green background and started its countdown.

"What does this all mean?" Lask said raising his hands as if pleading for help. "This is no game. It looks like a way to clog our minds and scare us!"

"Can't you see?" said Definimos. "We are to analyze what has ruined the environment and supply alternate possibilities. But on Domandosempria, we have the technology to markedly affect the climate and ecology."

"But that is not the case here," I pointed out. "The two of you must address the problem at hand with the digital resources available."

"Then, we must use the interface to explore the various alterations to temperature, types of energy, fuel supplies and the behavior of individuals that will prevent the catastrophe from occurring," said Definimos. "As Samuel said, we must input a positive plan, even though a complete solution may not be possible for quite some time given the parameters of the situation."

"To think of all these things would make us ill, and who knows if this is just to trick us to think what we saw is true when it is not," said Lask. "Big change makes big pain."

"We don't have time for this bickering!" I said. "You must compromise as you did before. See the clock. We must present a timely plan, or else we will fail the tests like the others before us."

Lask and Definimos were quiet for a moment as they appeared to try and collect their thoughts. The talkative Definimos was the first to approach the touchscreens.

"Actually, this could be quite entertaining. Here, I will decrease fossil fuel acquisition and usage by twenty-five per cent over thirty years," he said as he scrolled through the projected figures. "Of course, that means we must adjust the power grids and increase the alternative fuel sources there. Hmm, then we will have to ensure that expansion of these resources does not upset the ecosystem which could harm indigenous animal and plant life. So, we must calculate the size of preserved areas. You know there are no absolute answers here. It's all full of variables ..."

"May The Code save me!" shouted Lask. "You waste time. And all of this may just be fake. A test to see if we will stay on a safe path. Your plan will force quick change on this world and speed its end."

"Typical Burc," said Definimos. "Just believing what you want to believe. Never wanting to open the mind to alternate possibilities as to how to live. You would have the scenario we just saw play out just so you can put your life on autopilot and snooze until you crash into a mountain."

"We're getting nowhere here," I said. "Lask, I think if there is a connection between your two peoples, as The Safe suggests, I don't think who designed it wished to dismiss one of those worlds. Why not assume that you must deal with the catastrophe it presents. Definimos, we must present an answer, and not go down the rabbit hole of possibilities."

The two looked at each other and, without any acknowledgement, approached the video screens. Definimos performed triage to identify the worst elements destroying the ecosystem that needed immediate attention. He targeted those fuels and machines that caused pollution. Meanwhile, Lask chose a miscellaneous portal that allowed him to have planet leaders transmit new rules by using nonverbal video images. These would simply and directly tell the population to adjust to changes in their daily routines that would act in tandem with the adjustments that Definimos implemented. Coordination was the key to success.

At one point, I tried to help Definimos speed up his entries. When I touched the screen, a low-sounding, brief alarm emanated from the device. The screen froze and there appeared a video model of a DNA molecule followed by a red line diagonally drawn through it, as if to cancel it out.

"Apparently, your genetic make-up precludes you from directly participating," said Definimos. "Even though the technology here is very old, it is also quite advanced. Admirable."

After that, I stood by for the most part, anxiously looking at the clock as its face became whiter with the passing of time. I started to ask myself why I had put myself in such jeopardy for these two warring factions. Suppose they didn't complete the task in time? Why did I risk having my memories erased when I had serious doubts that these hugely different races would ever stop their violence toward each other? Yet part of me still wanted to accomplish something here. And, there was this feeling in the recesses of my being that hoped if something positive could be achieved here then maybe there was a chance that the people of Earth could find the ability to weld the cracks in its social fissures.

I then thought of Arthur. When I was in middle school and became distraught over trying to solve a problem, he would tell me to close the application I was working on. He told me to close my eyes, breathe deeply, and he would read a poem to me. I remember him reciting "The Dalliance of Eagles," by Walt Whitman, and "The Emperor of Ice Cream," by Wallace Stevens. His voice in my head calmed me then and now.

Lask stopped drawing his schematics and backed away from the screens. I saw Definimos sway back and forth as if the mental forces generated by the conflicting problems and solutions he was confronting were buffeting him. He hesitated, then took a deep breath as if to tap an internal energy source that allowed him to retreat from further investigation into more possible variations, and then pulled his hands away from the screens. I looked at my watch, which showed that almost four hours of Earth time had elapsed. The two men retreated to where I stood as the clock turned completely white and three chimes sounded. The display with their inputs again vanished and the spotlight illuminated a portal which opened to the next chamber. We collectively expelled sighs of relief and moved forward together.

Chapter Twenty-Six

We walked down a ramp that descended into the next room, which duplicated the appearance of the previous ones, and the clock again gave us time to eat and rest. I looked at my quiet companions and decided that these two new friends of mine needed to see the individuals behind the outward appearances of their enemies.

"How are Og and Pots?" I asked Lask. "I hope I did not cause them pain. Is Pots still to be wed?"

Lask shook his head in an almost slow-motion movement, as if weighed down by sadness.

"No," he said. "His mate-to-be will not join with one stained by too much thought. It is just as well; I did not like her much. He will see that she was not right for him."

"I am sad for him, though," I said, and I squeezed Lask's arm which reflected the tightness I felt in my chest. "How is Og?"

"She is smart," Lask said, smiling. "She acts as if all you said to her was wrong so as not to need the Cure. But she, and I, are glad you were there to help her with her thoughts."

"Has your spouse been helpful with the children?" asked Definimos.

"She is gone," replied Lask in a flat voice.

I decided to delve a little deeper into Lask's loss. "I know her name was Lure, but you have not said much of her."

Lask rubbed his small forehead and then said, "Lure was a sweet Burc. She showed warmth to me, Pots and Og. She did what The Code said, but knew when to bend it to help those who felt pain from its laws. She would help those who had their minds wiped, taught them to sew, cook, build, and clean once more. She did not judge them, but just felt sad for them."

There was a pause while we joined in Lask's sorrow.

"How did she die?" asked the curious Definimos.

"She had a growth here," said Lask, pointing to his chest. "It was cut out but it came back and spread. There was no way to stop it."

"I wish she had been on my planet," said Definimos. "We have made great strides in medicine. We could have cured her. If your people were more interested in taking care of their own instead of destroying mine, you could have applied your abilities to healing instead of killing."

Lask stood up, glared down at Definimos, and said with a voice almost choked with emotion, "If your world is so smart, why does it go out of its way to end our lives."

Lask walked toward the edge of the chamber, his back to us. I looked at Definimos, shook my head in disapproval, and raised my hands to suggest that Definimos say something to make amends for his hurtful words.

"I am sorry, Lask," he said. "You are right. My people have been recklessly destructive. You and your family have been very brave despite your suffering."

Lask turned around and quietly said, "As are you."

After a pause to let this exchange soak in, I decided to steer the conversation into brighter territory. I did not want to struggle with my lack of proficiency in the Burc language so I spoke in English and let the hub do the translating

"Lask, why don't you tell Definimos about your delicious recipes, and how much I helped in preparing them."

"Ha!" said Lask. "Don't give this man a knife. He will chop off parts of you if you get too close!"

We laughed, and Lask then related how awful I was at preparing one of the fowl dishes, trying to chop a piece of the meat and losing control of the cleaver, letting it fly off the table. We then traded descriptions of our favorite meals from our respective worlds. I told them one of my favorite desserts was the carrot cake my mother used to make and described its ingredients.

"Seems odd," said Lask, squinting his eyes. "It's not right to mix a sweet with a plant."

"We have something like that on Domandosempria," said Definimos. "I agree with Lask. I don't like it. But, at least I have tried it."

Lask bobbed his head from side to side, weighing the possibility.

"Well, one day, you may make it for me," he said to me.

"Yes," I said. "One day."

There was a pause and then Definimos said, "Was your mother a good cook?"

"Yes. She was good at many things," I said. "She was a great dancer, and could play the piano. She would perform on holidays for the family and at special events at the school where she taught. She passed on her affection for science to me. I wish she could have been with me longer."

"She is still with you," said Lask, and I nodded my head in agreement.

We decided to take a short nap before the next task. But, I had trouble staying asleep, as I worried about the consequences of what would happen to us if the mission was a failure. Even if some of the events I experienced were negative, they were still my memories and belonged to me, and I would be less of who I am if they were wiped away.

The three gong alarms sounded and with a combination of anticipation and dread we ascended the platform, initiating the next display. Shifting images showed scenes of the humanoid animations in a room, fiercely gesturing at each other and pointing to maps, as if quarreling over some land. Those on one side of the conflict had long arms, while those on the opposing side had short upper appendages. One leader pointed to a list of abstract figures projected on the wall on his side of the area while an opposing chieftain waved toward his own display. The scene shifted to public rallies where youths, with the assistance of adults who may have been their parents, burned images of the individuals of those with opposing viewpoints and different sized upper extremities. There were then displays of armies dressed in distinct colors, one in red, the other in blue. The two sides fired weapons at each other as soldiers fell to the ground either dead or wounded. The next video showed patient-filled hospitals as medical professionals on both fronts tried to treat the casualties as the soldiers screamed in agony while bleeding as medics brought in more of the combatants from the battlefields. Spacecraft showered towns below with explosives that evaporated parts of populated areas. What I saw penetrated my eyes like visual bullets, rendering me emotionally wounded. Lask and Definimos turned away at some of the horrific sights, especially those that depicted children as victims.

What followed was a loud and brilliant explosion which caused us to close our eyes and cover our ears. When the blast was over, what remained was a devastated landscape with an immense dark cloud hovering over it. Nothing moved or grew on the desolate ground. A large black "X" then appeared over the dead world.

The screen then turned white followed by groupings of icons that depicted the two races in various settings, including hospitals, schools, and public meetings, among others. Then the clock on the wall started its countdown.

"Obviously, we must devise a plan that will ease the sufferings of these people and put an end to the destructive confrontation between them," said Definimos.

"Obviously," said the smiling Lask, whose taunting use of the multi-syllabic word brought reciprocal smiles from Definimos and me. Lask then became serious. "First we must have the two tribes join to stop the fight so both sides can treat those hurt, the young ones first."

"Excellent!" said Definimos. "Then we must have meetings to work out an extended cease-fire so that each side compromises on its demands concerning resources, land boundaries, and safety."

"Then the schools must teach to not hate those that are not the same as them," added Lask.

"And respect those differences so long as the beliefs of either side are not a threat to the others," said Definimos.

I looked at the two men and nodded.

"It appears that both of you have already given a great deal of thought about this topic," I said. "You don't need my help."

I sat and watched as Lask and Definimos manipulated the interactive displays. It was not an easy task. Several times when they moved icons to present possible solutions the large "X" would appear accompanied by a buzzer, indicating the annihilation of the factions, thus invalidating their suggestions, and they had to make adjustments. At various times they just stopped from exhaustion and sat down momentarily while the clock face continued to change from green to white. I brought them water and food as they persisted in their endeavor to beat the clock. They collaborated more on this task than before, asking each other for advice. They began to speed up as they neared the completion of the simulation. My heart began to race as I feared they would not reach the goal. Again, they finished just before their time was up.

Darkness engulfed us once more, and again we held our breaths, hoping that we could move forward with our memories intact. A light emblazoned the entrance to the next room, the door to it slid open, and we allowed ourselves some deep breaths to ease our constricted lungs.

"If there are more tests, I may have to break some things," said the weary Lask.

Chapter Twenty-Seven

The chamber, again lower than the one that preceded it, had a stage and a clock as did the others. But, here there were two large purple discs on either side of the raised platform. Lask looked at the setting and gave out a groan while Definimos smiled and simply shook his bowed head. We were again given time to rest and tend to our bodily needs. Afterwards, Lask and Definimos took deep breaths and then ascended the stage, triggering another holographic display. It was a short but disturbing piece of enactment. Two figures appeared behind a lit barrier on the platform. This virtual wall sparkled, as if it was a sort of electrified fence. The two digital projections approached a generated starting line. One figure moved past the other prematurely before an alarm signaling the start of what appeared to be a race. When he came into contact with the wall he was propelled backwards. The alarm sounded again, and this time both figures ran together toward the opposite wall and the electronic barrier disappeared. One of the runners reached a disc before the other and pressed it. Another alarm rang out. The figure that did not reach the other disc had to endure the mind wipe.

We all looked at each other, astonished, and then Lask vented his outrage.

"We have done all of this and one of us must still be harmed?" he said.

"It does point to a conclusion," observed Definimos. "This test, or whatever it is we have been doing, was meant for two people to endure. When only one of your Procs participated, there was no chance to finish even if he or she reached this point."

I tried to rev up my problem-solving abilities to figure out what was supposed to happen and wondered how to prevent one of my new friends from having The Safe erase his memories.

"It makes no sense," I said. "Both of you, together, using your individual skills, were able to get this far. Why would this place punish one of you just because he was the second to reach the button?"

I pondered for a moment, searching for a safe haven amid my mental storm. I found none.

"It is illogical!" I yelled. "Cooperation was what was most important here. Why make the two of you turn against each other now?"

Definimos rubbed his expanded forehead as he pondered what I said.

"Maybe we really aren't supposed to compete," he said. "Maybe that is the real test."

Lask looked at him and his small eyes widened.

"Yes," Lask said. "It may be that we should both win."

"How can that be?" I said, feeling some hope at last.

"We run to the disc devices, but we press them simultaneously," said Definimos.

"Why can't you just say, 'at the same time,'" said Lask with eyes rolling.

I was unsure of this plan.

"How do you know that will work?" I asked. "You may lock each other out and be forced to perform the task again," I said. "Or, you may both be subjected to the mind erasure. There isn't enough evidence to make a definitive choice. We require more information."

"I delight in your desire to know more," said Definimos. "But sometimes time will not allow us to satisfy our inquisitiveness. On occasion, we must stop thinking and just act."

"At last, we see things the same," said Lask.

Definimos and Lask reached the starting line. The signal to begin the race sounded. They ran toward the discs, with Lask arriving first. However, he refrained from pressing the disc. When Definimos arrived at the other round button on the wall a moment later, the two men looked at each other. Lask spoke.

"On three," he said, "One, two ... three!"

The two men pressed the discs at the same time. The chamber went dark. I could see nothing at all and began to tremble out of fear of the unknown, not having a clue as to what to expect from the improvised action of Lask and Definimos. Would The Safe wipe all three of our minds and keep its secrets locked up?

I heard a hydraulic sound and then saw that a portal slid open between the two men. Light flooded in through the gateway, illuminating the room in which we stood motionless. I then approached Lask and Definimos. We smiled at each other indicating our relief. We then proceeded through the opening.

Chapter Twenty-Eight

Unlike the other chambers, the entrance to this room slanted upwards. The enclosure was circular and domed. A golden hue bathed the space. There was another stage here, and we climbed onto it. On the platform was a cone-shaped pillar which had a button in its middle. Definimos pressed it and a virtual reality projection appeared on the platform. The image was of a room with many computer-generated individuals who resembled humans more than Burcs or Domandosemprians. The beings formed two groups, and they shouted at each other. Those on the right had somewhat smaller heads than people on Earth. On the left were individuals whose heads were slightly more prominent than the size of my own.

One of those on the left held up a binder and opened it. He pointed to a document contained inside. One individual on the right had what appeared to be a duplicate binder and began to rip parts of the text out.

"The scrolls have words like old Burc," said Lask as he walked close to the display. "That looks like The Code!"

He deciphered some of it and became excited. "The one on the left starts with the names of those who wrote it, which we do not have. It talks of how some felt the need to write rules as there were those that thought too much, and this brought a split."

"It sounds like the original Code was a sort of history of your people," I said to Lask. He thought for a moment and then nodded.

The projection changed and there were images of bloody battles fought between the two factions. There were explosions, decimated buildings, and images of hospitals with numerous patients. There were also scenes of cemeteries with row upon row of graves.

In the end those with the smaller heads prevailed. What followed were a series of videos showing how the smaller heads deleted references to the background of their people and added additional provisions into their history. They then incarcerated those with larger heads, erased their memories, and loaded them onto a spacecraft. The winners then proceeded to wipe their own memories.

"Why did they do that?" asked Lask.

"I believe it was to erase facts concerning their aberrant fellow citizens to prevent too much knowledge that might encourage questioning," said Definimos.

The projection then showed a large group of smaller and larger heads escaping the mind-erasing by hiding out together in caves in the wilderness. They had the copy of The Code before the editing. There were then scenes of this coalition building The Safe. This renegade group commandeered their own spaceship and fled. The projection displayed the coordinates of the planet where they were headed.

"I believe they placed that prior section of Burc history here to show proof at a later time of the origins of both of your societies. Did you record those coordinates?" I asked Definimos.

"Of course, "he said, "I used the memory function on the translator to store as proof what we are witnessing."

The last image of the VR projection had two members of this rebellious group, one with a smaller head and one with a larger, smiling with welcoming waving hands, as if beckoning the viewers to visit them.

The three of us stared at each other speechless. After the projection ended, the wall behind the stage slowly parted and encased in some type of plastic laminate was a document. Lask approached the artifact slowly with reverence.

"The first part of The Code," he whispered, "which has been lost to us for so long."

Definimos used his translator to decipher the large amount of writing in the old Burc tongue. He read its contents and relayed what it said to Lask and me. There were names that Lask believed referred to the Gens that ruled Burc a long time ago and who wrote the history of Burc before the editing and added rules of The Code. It related details of what we observed which fit the notion of the Great Quake that Lask referred to when I first began to learn about Burc's past.

There was another inscription below The Code. It was in old Burc. Definimos used the translator to scan the words. The interpretation said the allies made The Safe as proof of the origins of the natives for when the time was right for reunification to take place. They designed the visuals in the prior chambers to communicate the scenarios of the tests to the descendants of both factions.

The translation added that there had been an evolutionary change which led to some Burcs developing the slightly larger brain matter. They fought against the existing establishment. The prevailing ancient Burcs exiled those "mutants," who secretly carried with them, before their mind wipe, an image that symbolized the planet's evolution, a sculpture of a bird with curved wings that sits on a line and ends in a triangle. The same image that the coalition of smaller and larger head rebels carved into The Safe before their escape.

"That was how we received the image. My people came from here!" said Definimos. "Can it truly be?"

"The Burc leaders revised the original Code to simplify the language and turn it into its current state," I said. "And, I am guessing that those on the planet where the escapees went consist of who you call Syntharmians."

Lask was silent for a moment and then nodded his head in agreement, and Definimos said, "I think your hypothesis is a reasonable one."

There was silence for a while before Definimos spoke again.

"It is obvious what we must do," he said. "Lask and I must somehow bring this information to our respective peoples. It will be difficult to overcome entrenched prejudices, but we need to show them that we must not tolerate war against one's own family."

Lask nodded his consent. He then reached for The Code and was able to extract it from its base. After he did so, a door opened on the edge of the circular room. Light came through that did not seem artificial. We approached the opening together. Stairs led upward and we scaled them. At the top there was a transparent hatch that was secured from the inside. There were outlines of two sets of hands on the hatch.

"I believe each of you needs to place your hands on one of the interfaces," I said.

Definimos and Lask did as I recommended. The hatch opened. We climbed out to the surface. A rock formation encircled the hatch. It prevented detection from anyone passing by. The barrier, however, was scalable.

"Well, my friend," said Definimos, addressing me, "we know what our task is. What will you do now?"

"I suppose I must go with you two to help convince your citizens of what we have learned," I said.

"I don't think that is necessary," said Definimos. "We have enough information for those who are willing to listen."

"I think he is right," said Lask. "You must do what is right for you now."

I thought for a moment, which was shorter than the usual amount of time when I pondered a problem.

"Since I am here on Burc, I will go with you to address the Burc Proc Group. After that, I'm going to the third planet," I said.

Chapter Twenty-Nine

We climbed over the rugged, red rocks that hid the hatch, getting a few scrapes along the way, and rejoined AM who remained at the entrance to The Safe. He was in a powered-down mode but became activated as we approached. He observed Lask carrying the ancient portion of The Code.

"It appears that your efforts were successful, since you now possess an artifact that I assume came from The Safe," AM said.

"Yes, but we have a challenging time ahead of us," said a solemn Definimos. "There will be a delay in returning to Domandosempria."

"We will go to my hut first," Lask said. "I will set up a time to share what we have found. I will say that I have a thing of great worth to Burc. You will need cloaks to hide who you two are."

Lask pointed to some furry brown clothing that he brought with him.

"You do mean the three of us, don't you, sir?" said AM "I hope I will not be left behind once again."

"Yes, we will need AM," I said. "He has evidence of the bird symbol on Domandosempria that will back up our argument. You're capable of sharing the image, right AM?"

"Absolutely," responded AM. "I am fully functional in sharing my accumulated knowledge, down to the smallest detail."

"Let us hope it does not come to that," said Lask.

After I, Definimos, and AM disguised ourselves, we rode the tram, dodging any sinkholes along the way. When we reached Lask's hut, he contacted One, the Top Proc, and set up a meeting with him alone, thinking that a gathering with all the Procs at once would be overwhelming and dangerous. We then traveled to the Hub and, due to Lask's authoritative position, he was able to schedule the meeting with the Top Proc in the leader's private office. It was spare and made of stone and metal like many of the rooms on Burc. However, as in Lask's hut, there were multiple surveillance monitors mounted on the walls. The Top Proc entered from a sliding door at the rear of the room. His body was bent forward, and he moved almost in slow motion, with labored breathing as he inhaled short intakes of air. It seemed it would not be long before he would succumb to his illness. He hesitated when he saw that Lask was not alone, but he then proceeded to the chair behind his granite-like desk. Definimos used his translator disc to interpret the Burc language for himself and handed Lask an earpiece, who gave it to the Top Proc. He at first held it at a distance, which looked like he was afraid it would infect him. He saw that Lask also used one and then he hesitantly inserted it into his ear. AM was able to use the interpreting application contained in his neural net.

"So, what have you to tell me?" he asked. "I hope it is what will help and not harm us."

Lask opened a large canvas bag he carried and pulled out the plastic-encased portion of The Code he secured from The Safe. He opened it and handed it to the Top Proc.

"You know what this is," he said. "The same words that are on the arch to The Safe are here, too. The words show it to be the lost part of The Code we long for."

The Top Proc looked afraid to hold the object offered to him, as if it would burn him for having the audacity to touch it.

"It states the names of the Gens and talks of the Great Quake and the need for The Code," said Lask.

The Top Proc scanned the document and then looked at Lask.

"How did you get this?" he asked.

"It is from The Safe," said Lask. "We went there and brought back the truth about us and our foes."

"Who are 'we?'" came the next question from the Top Proc.

"Show who you are," said Lask.

We removed our hooded cloaks, eliciting a strained gasp from the Burc leader.

"What have you done?" said the Top Proc, stressing each of his words. He rose from his seat. "How dare you join with those who seek to end us!"

"Not all wish to do so," said Lask. "Some, such as Definimos here, want an end to the death, to the war."

"You speak his name like he is a friend," said the Top Proc, his face scrunched like he tasted something bitter. "You should feel pain when you say who he is."

Lask ignored his leader's anger and set about making his case.

"The key to bring back what we have looked for was on the door to The Safe," he said. "It says that peace comes when one joins with the foe. To do that means we must know our past. With the help of the Domandosemprian and Sam the thore, we came out of The Safe with what it had to tell us."

"You lie," said the Top Proc, shaking his head. "The Code says we must fight those who try to change our ways."

"You know just part of what took place," said Lask. "The bot, which can't lie, will show what we tell you is not made up."

AM moved forward and provided details of the symbol on Domandosempria and its history. He also projected in a hologram the digital interface he made of the recording that Definimos created of the events that took place in The Safe. After AM concluded his report, the Top Proc, who had stared down at the desk during AM's testimony, looked up and aimed his eyes at us. He repeatedly shook his head as if expressing an ongoing "no," and his facial features tightened, suggesting the fortifying of a wall against anything that might attack his perception of reality.

"All that was said is fake," he pronounced. "I do not know of this bot, but it comes from our foe, and was made to lie."

"I do not wish to contradict you, sir, but your allegations are outrageous," said AM. "I have a 99.99 percent accuracy rating, and the only reason it is not one hundred per cent is because my technology is not capable of perceiving everything. But, as you can guess, I am far superior in my observations compared to any organic creature."

The Top Proc ignored the mechanical and said, "There is no old bond that joins our worlds. Our foes want to get close to us so that they can take what we have and ruin us."

"That is not true!" declared Definimos. "I was as outraged at this connection as you are. But we must face the facts, and not continue to believe what we held as true just because it was all we knew. We can't throw out information if it doesn't fit what we are used to accepting as valid!"

The Top Proc pointed at Definimos and spoke.

"You have ruined one of our Procs with your false ways. You all must be cleansed of these thoughts so as not to spread the fake claims. And this (he held up the early version of The Code) must be burned!"

I dashed forward and grabbed the document out of the Top Proc's hand.

"Where I come from, we believed things for a long time that were false," I said. "We thought our home planet was the center of the universe and everything else revolved around it. But scientists gave us facts that proved our views were wrong. The same happened when almost everyone thought our world was flat, until we explored and revealed the truth that it was almost spherical in nature. Our medicine was once based on unverified conclusions that different liquids, called humors, controlled our bodies. If someone became ill, we bled them supposedly to put the liquids in balance. Scientific investigation has discovered the true causes of various sicknesses, and now treatment is highly successful. Over and over the need to question our beliefs has been necessary to stop us from going down an ignorant and harmful path."

The Top Proc sneered at me and said, "You told us that your world is still in the throes of war, greed, and pain. How dare you tell us how to live."

Definimos realized that understanding at the most, and compromise at the least, was unattainable.

"AM, neutralize," he said.

AM's movement was like a blur as he moved behind the Top Proc and inflicted his version of the Vulcan nerve pinch, using his upper appendages to squeeze the back of the Top Proc's neck, rendering him unconscious.

"Others may come and will see what we have done and will take us. We must leave here through the door from which he joined us. I know the way," said Lask.

We followed him through the sliding door which led to the Top Proc's private office.

"I think we must go back to my hut," said Lask. "I must warn Og and Pots that bots may come to wipe their minds. The Procs might think the two of them know what I know, and see them as threats."

"After that," I said, "We must get to my ship, and I will take the three of you to Domandosempria. Hopefully there we will have greater success in stopping this war."

Even as Definimos, AM and I recloaked ourselves before leaving the room, I felt an emptiness inside of me. I knew on Earth people with entrenched views rarely rose above their mired ideas to build bridges to the beliefs of others. I hoped that I was part of a better resolution here.

Chapter Thirty

We made our way into the Top Proc's office through a narrow corridor. Lask checked outside the door of the room and after confirming that the walkway was safe for us, he waived us through the portal. I was afraid that we would be found out, and the thought of having my mind wiped clean caused me to start sweating. The hood covering my head did not help, and I wiped my face. Definimos noted my elevated stress level.

"You must remain calm," he said. "Our worlds are relying on you."

Well, that made me feel much better. Despite my Domandosemprian friend piling on the pressure, I was able to access a memory of my childhood, when I pretended to be a superhero who could fly in the sky. I was able to visualize soaring away from this place and took some deep breaths which eased my tension.

As we made our way to the exit where we left the tram, a loud, repetitive gong began to sound.

"They must have found the Top Proc!" Lask told us. "We must be quick!"

We sped up our movement through the last walkway and rushed toward the tram. After we were on board Lask accelerated the vehicle to its top speed in a couple of seconds.

Lask pursed his lips and took some deep breaths. He then nodded, it seemed to himself, as if he had made up his mind.

"There is no time for me to go to my hut and get in touch with Og and Pots," he said "It was known I met with the Top Proc. The Procs will send bots to come for me and who is with me."

We looked at each other, and slowly nodded our heads, even AM. Lask used his communication device to contact Og and tell her that she and her brother must flee and hide. We heard Og sobbing as she heard her father's words.

"We will go to Kinth's place," said Og. "She is a good friend. I have talked with her, and she has some of the same thoughts that I do. She has a room in the ground close to her hut where we can hide. I love you. Please be safe."

"I love you too, dear one," said Lask, and his hand shook a little as he held the communications wand. "Give my love to Pots."

We were quiet for a moment to give Lask time to deal with the decision to leave his children for the good of his planet.

"I am sorry that you will be leaving your family behind," said Definimos. "I have done the same, and hopefully we will both be reunited with those we love soon."

It was then Lask's turn to nod his head in agreement. I guided Lask to the large out-cropping of rock where I hid the Seeker and, soon after, I retrieved the HOPS transducer. I warned Lask of the effect that the Seeker's navigation system may have on him. He stoically waved his hand quickly, as if dismissing any problem that might occur. I took off and as I headed out of the Burc atmosphere, a deep vibrating sound penetrated the area near us, and the Seeker shook from its vibration. I knew it was the Burc weapon. I altered the course of the Seeker as far as I could away from the weapon's acoustic blast and initiated the HOPS drive with coordinates for Domandosempria just as we heard the increasing volume of another attack approach us.

After the conversion from wave to matter, I saw that Domandosempria was in view. The feeling of relief that we made it away from Burc did not last long as Lask began to shriek as he reverted to his pre-flight form. He was shaking and his eyes were wide with pupils dilated. I went to the first aid kit I stored on board and checked his vital signs. His heart rate was accelerated and his blood pressure was elevated, at least by human standards. I offered him a sedating tea I brought with me from Burc in the hope of calming the usually even-tempered Lask. After several minutes his agitation subsided.

"Do you feel fine now?" I asked him.

"Yes," Lask said. "But the flight scared me. I saw and heard things that no Burc should deal with."

I gave Lask some water which he almost inhaled. He told us that he had visions of mathematical equations that needed solving projected on walls. He saw Burcs discussing books containing enigmatic stories. He heard voices analyzing scientific theories about the origins and future of the universe. He described envisioning musical and dramatic perfor-mances with strange sounds and displays that I could only describe as being avant-garde.

"All was in flux," said Lask. "All the Burcs had their own thoughts on how to be. Too much, too much."

"Welcome to my world," said Definimos.

"I do not think I could live there, "said Lask.

"As I could not survive on Burc," noted Definimos.

There was a brief silence before I spoke.

"Perhaps someday you both will find a way to make each other's worlds hospitable for the other," I said.

"Would you like to hear the odds of that happening?" asked AM.

The three of us responded with a resounding, "No!"

"In the meantime," I said, "let's try to at least stop your planets' inhabitants from trying to kill each other."

I set down the Seeker on the outskirts of Darnounoby, to a spot Definmos said was desolate. Definimos told us it would be best if he approached the Governing Brain Trust alone. He felt that seeing Lask could invoke the prejudice against the Burcs which was strong despite the openness to new ideas that the Domandosemprians professed. He said he would take The Code and AM with him to try and convince the Trust of the ancient link between the two races. We would be close by in disguise.

"I will try to make the argument that when we kill a Burc, we are eliminating one of our own relatives," said Definimos. "I am hoping for a ceasefire while they review the evidence, and that the Trust will use me as an emissary to reach a cessation of hostilities. It is then that I will introduce Lask to show that we already have a Burc leader who is willing to negotiate peace."

After a brief silence Lask said, "It is worth a try. But, I have grave doubts that it will work."

Chapter Thirty-One

A M used his interface with the other mechanicals to bring a hovercraft to us. We traveled to the Great Hall and stayed hooded in our vehicle in the event any Domandosemprians noticed us. Before Definimos and AM left to enter the building, Definimos spoke to Lask and me.

"Think of us as being on a grand quest, an adventure to exert significant change in our lives. It's quite exciting!"

Lask grunted.

"What would please me would be to be in my hut, in my warm bed," he said, adding, "Alone."

Definimos, getting used to his grumpy companion, just laughed, and said, "I hope I will return triumphantly!"

After Definimos and AM left us, I turned to Lask and said, "You said the word 'alone.' Two sounds."

Lask wrapped his arms around his upper body, as if fortifying himself.

"See," he said, "I must be on guard. Soon he will have long words burst out of me."

Despite my attempt to lighten Lask's mood, I was feeling dejected about our attempts to secure a ceasefire between Domandosempria and Burc. I was experiencing déjà vu, as if the wars between differing peoples on Earth were being replayed throughout the galaxy. The two of us were quiet for a period before I spoke.

"Do you think peace can come and heal your two worlds?" I asked.

"I do not know," said Lask, staring ahead. "I'm not sure if we can join as we once were in past times." He looked at me. "But we must try."

We lapsed into silence again and eventually dozed off for a while. We heard something familiar that jarred us awake. It was a deep vibrating sound followed by the crumbling of a building in the distance. We looked at each other.

"A Burc ship," said Lask.

Before we could seek shelter, Definimos appeared in the hovercraft with AM.

"The worst timing for your people to be belligerent," he said to Lask. "I was presenting the evidence and making my argument. Even though Nadatermincos continued his bellicose stance against the Burcs, I believe I was convincing the others that, as is our nature, we should be open to new possibilities. But then this attack! I am not sure I will be able to win them over."

"Less talk now!" said Lask. "We can make plans soon. First, we must be safe."

"Yes, of course," said Definimos. "I need to go to my home. I must ensure the protection of my family. AM, take us there!"

Chapter Thirty-Two

Our hovercraft arrived at the home of Definimos as the planet's defenses repelled the Burc attack, which soon ended. Pansapianna was waiting for us, and she tightly embraced Definimos. I saw Lask nodding, acknowledging the affection the two showed each other. When one does not see an enemy at a distance and witnesses that they share basic needs, it is difficult to want your foes to suffer.

"Where are the children?" asked Definimos.

"They are at their school, safe in a shelter," said Pansapianna. "I have been in contact with them through the viewer. Do you want to talk with them?

Definimos excused himself and Pansapianna accompanied him to the bedroom to remotely reassure his children. Lask observed the living quarters. He leaned next to me and spoke quietly.

"Not at all what I am used to," he said. "See-through floors?"

I smiled.

"It would be hard for me to get used to them, too," I said. "On that we are of one mind."

Pansapianna returned and stared at Lask, who looked away, apparently feeling uncomfortable. She also noted his aversion to scrutinization.

"I apologize," she said. "I have never seen a Burc in person. I guess it is difficult for either of us to feel relaxed around each other, given how different we appear, and all that has transpired between our two worlds."

"I see you share your mate's urge to talk a great deal," said Lask. I gave him a stern look, which he observed.

"I did not mean to be rude," he said. "Yes, it is hard for us to deal with our past and the way we are."

Definimos rejoined us and informed his wife of what happened in The Safe. Lask told her of our difficulty in trying to convince the Top Proc to accept the history involving both worlds. Pansapianna listened with her mouth and eyes wide open, as if trying to take in this amazing information. She held onto a chair to steady herself before speaking.

"I believe you must bypass the leaders," she said. "They are entrenched in their powerful roles. You must inform the people of both planets of the evidence you have discovered. Once you convince them of the truth then those who resist will have to capitulate."

We looked at each other for a moment, realizing the task Pansapianna presented to us.

"I think she's right," I said, knowing from my own experiences on Earth that a motivated population could bring about change.

"Yes, it appears to be the best way," said Definimos. "But you must leave Domandosempria, Samuel. If Nadatermincos and his followers discover your spacecraft is here, he may convince others that they can adapt it as a weapon to win the war. I will give you translators so you can communicate with the Syntharmians. They deserve to know that we are endeavoring to join them one day."

He stopped for a moment, as if taking time to decide. He nodded to himself.

"Also, take AM with you," he said. "He can be quite useful, verifying what we experienced. It also seems that you have bonded with him, so you two will be compatible on your journey. I can upload what he has recorded to another auxiliary mechanical."

AM, who had been content to just follow orders silently, felt the need to speak up.

"Indeed, Samuel," he said, "all mechanicals can share data with the utmost accuracy. And I would be very willing to assist you in your journey. I excel at navigation and at interpreting a variety of sensory inputs. I hope I am not bragging too much."

"They all speak so much," Lask muttered, covering his ears.

"No problem," I said to AM, and smiled. "Very reassuring."

Definimos used a portable drive to download AM's data memory so that he could input it secretly into another mechanical. Then, Definimos, Lask and AM accompanied me in the hovercraft to the spot where I landed the Seeker in the frontier near Darnounoby.

"I am sad to say goodbye to both of you, especially when you have so much work to do," I said.

"I must admit that I will miss your investigative and sharp mind," said Definimos. "Without your help we could not even conceive of the possibility of an end to hostilities. I thank you, as does my family, and I am sure, eventually, my people."

Lask cringed as he listened to Definimos. "Nice to have met you," he said. "I wish you well."

"We have the coordinates for Syntharm now," said Definimos. "Once we are successful on showing the connection between Burc and Domandosempria, we will visit our distant relatives."

Definimos also programmed AM with secure hailing frequencies to contact him if we were close enough to communicate in the future. After giving both Lask and Definimos hugs, I secured the hidden transducer. I then entered my spacecraft along with AM. As I prepared the ship for takeoff, AM asked me a question.

"Samuel, do you think I will again experience those waves of electrical impulses flooding my sensors, those nonquantifiable 'emotions,' as you called them?"

"It's possible," I said. "You may have some sweet dreams."

AM cocked his head to one side. "I don't see how anything in my circuitry could have a sugary taste," he said.

"It's just an expression," I said with a smile. "Let's just say I hope your electrical impulses are positive ones."

"Hmm," said AM, considering what I said. "I wish the same for you."

Part Four

Syntharm

Chapter Thirty-Three

I entered the stellar location of Syntharm into the navigation system, and both I and AM secured ourselves. I enabled the HOPS and the mass-to-wave transformation took place. The Seeker then initiated the wormhole effect, and I began having visions as we flowed through space. It seemed to me that the universe began to shapeshift as planets turned into gases and then reformed again. I saw what looked like humanoids of varied sizes alter and merge. I caught a glimpse of myself in an embrace with a woman. However, I felt frustrated trying to discern what I visualized since everything looked hazy, as if I was viewing images through a blurring mist. Our trip was farther than the distance between Burc and Domandosempria, but Syntharm was relatively close compared to the vast distance from Earth.

After converting back to our well-defined forms, I was curious to find out if AM could provide more insight into the conversion.

"What can you report concerning your journey this time?" I asked the mechanical.

AM looked straight ahead and was still for a moment. I assumed he was accessing his data files.

"I must say that my input from the experience is conflicting," AM said. "I recorded indistinct pixels and discordant sounds. Everything seemed to fluctuate. I am sorry to say I have nothing conclusive to convey. Most disconcerting."

"I know how you feel," I said.

I checked the Seeker's sensors, but they did not detect Syntharm nearby. Instead, the ship's alert notification system reported that there was an asteroid field before us. I turned on the outside viewer, but I could not discern a planet in sight. I double-checked the coordinates I entered. I became agitated.

"I don't understand," I said, shaking my head. "I was exact in my input. Why isn't it here?"

"Perhaps I may be of assistance," said AM. "I have tracking components that are superior to those in your craft."

AM hesitated for a moment.

"I am not trying to act superior to your technology," AM said. "I am merely attempting to provide helpful information."

"It's fine." I was impatient and said, "Don't worry about that. Just do what you can to find our destination."

AM seemed to go into a trance as he jacked one of his fiber optic digits into an auxiliary port which connected his scanning sensors to the Seeker. After several minutes, he became aware of my presence again.

"It is most confusing," said AM. "We have definitely arrived at the correct coordinates. I can detect some inconsistent subspace interference beyond our point, but it is inconclusive."

"What do you suggest we do?" I asked.

"Suggest?" said AM. "I am not used to expressing inexact recommendations."

"Make an exception this time," I said. "Extrapolate from what you observe. Make an educated guess."

AM rotated his head away from me and then back again.

"Make a guess," he said. "That sounds like a human action."

"Reach beyond your circumscribed components," I said. "Aspire to something greater than the mathematical exactness of your programming."

"Hmm," said AM. "That sounds like utilizing the human attribute of intuition."

"Give it a shot," I said. "I know you have it in you, AM."

AM resumed his trance-like state for a moment before exiting his contemplative mode.

"A 'shot?' I am not sure what you mean," said AM.

"You know, take a stab at it," I said.

"Why is your language so violent?" asked AM.

I thought for a second.

"It is, isn't it?" I said. "I guess even in our metaphors my people show how destructive we can be. In any event, I am just saying that you should propose a theory which expresses a possible explanation of the situation given the information you have."

"Very well," said AM, and he was silent while he analyzed the possibilities.

"Samuel," he said, "the data indicates that there might be something beyond our present location that does not correspond to asteroid formations. I hypothesize that there is some type of cloaking field before us. I would proceed forward – but carefully to avoid any collision in the event that my prediction is incorrect."

I activated the maneuvering thrusters and sent the Seeker toward the supposedly dangerous asteroid field. I wanted to believe that AM's prediction was correct, but that belief was under attack by my fear that we were approaching our doom. I began to sweat, and AM noticed.

"You are leaking, sir," he observed. "Should we alter the atmospheric levels to compensate?"

"No," I said. "It's just an emotional response."

"Hmm," AM said. "I have found emotions to be confusing to comprehend. I hope you do not dehydrate."

"Me, too," I said.

We proceeded. Maneuvering around the asteroids would be tricky, if not impossible. I took a chance at heading straight for one of the smaller cosmic bodies even though, according to the sensors, it registered mass readings.

"Goodness gracious," said AM, "do you think it is advisable to proceed on this path?"

"Looks like the only way to test your theory," I said.

My anxiety increased as we came close to the object before us, but instead of having dangerous contact with the rock formation, the Seeker passed right through it.

"It appears to be a sophisticated multi-dimensional holographic projection," I said. I turned to AM. "Very good prediction."

AM bowed his head in appreciation.

After advancing beyond the phony asteroids, the Seeker parted what turned out to be a transparent spatial curtain that began to shimmer as the craft penetrated it. When we were on the other side we observed a planet in the distance.

"Syntharm?" asked AM.

"I think so," I said.

Chapter Thirty-Four

As we approached a landing on Syntharm I observed that there were extensive fog formations covering the planet. I put the Seeker on autopilot since its guidance system was better than my own ability to avoid any hidden obstructions.

"Samuel," said AM, "may I assist your craft? I believe our combined abilities will ensure a safe landing."

"Knock yourself out," I said.

AM swiveled his dome-shaped head toward me. "Rendering myself inoperative would not be recommended," the android said.

"Sorry," I said. "That was another violent saying from my planet. It means that you should give it your best try."

"I believe you want me to succeed, not just try," said AM.

"Well, yes, of course," I said. "Humans try to succeed but are not always successful."

AM nodded his head and approached the main command panel. He again inserted one of his digits into the piloting console. When he secured the link, the rest of his mechanical arm lit up, as did his cranium.

"We should decorate you for Christmas," I said, and realized as soon as I made the reference to a holiday tree that there would be another misunderstanding.

"I have no need for a commendation for my actions, being a synthetic," AM said.

"I was making a reference to a tradition on Earth," I said. "We decorate a tree with lights, not awards, and other ornaments at the time some believe a deity was born."

"I do not see the relationship between something otherworldly and a tree," AM said.

"Forget it. Just put us down somewhere away from any occupied area you observe," I said.

We landed in a secluded open field. The atmosphere was similar to that on Earth, but richer in oxygen, which was a relief to me since I knew I could breathe without a spacesuit. The mass of the planet was less than that of Burc, so the gravity of this world was not as burdensome. It was closer to that of Earth's than the far less dense Domandosempria. Thick patches of either heavy fog or fine mist saturated the surface. I was worried that I might not be able to see an object right before I collided with it as I walked. The star that warmed the system that included Syntharm created a temperate climate. After exiting my craft, I found the sunlight a welcoming sensation whenever it shown through the moist covering. There was a forest to our rear and a flat plain in front of us, as well as I could tell given the decreased visibility.

"I believe we should head toward the end of the level surface," said AM. "I am picking up transmissions from that area that resemble increased electronic communication. It is possible the inhabitants have detected us."

I nodded and detached the propulsion transducer from the Seeker. I thought about hiding it, but reconsidered. "I'll just carry this with us in my backpack," I said to AM. "I think the inhabitants are trustworthy here."

"What makes you believe that is this case?" asked AM.

"That's what my gut is telling me," I said.

"I heard no utterances from any part of you except your mouth," said AM.

I laughed and said, "Let's get started."

We walked toward where we believed there was civilization. Moisture from the mist collected on my eyelids, and I wiped it off every so often so it wouldn't further cloud my vision. The atmosphere smelled damp, like grass after a deluge of rain has fallen.

"I hope I do not rust in this atmosphere," commented AM.

"You should have brought an oil can," I said.

AM again cocked his head toward me. "Oil can?" he asked.

"I apologize again. I was talking about a petroleum lubricant used on my planet," I said. "I was also making a reference to a famous story on Earth. There is a character called the Tin Man who rusts and needs others to oil him to move again."

"Hm," said AM, "The mechanicals on Domandosempria have routine maintenance to prevent deterioration. My calendar says that I am a bit overdue. What is this oil made from?"

"It's a fossil fuel derived from dead organisms," I said. "One would think it's a form of recycling, but its use pollutes the atmosphere."

"How odd and unevolved," said AM.

"Yes, I would have to agree," I said. "Anyway, the Tin Man in the tale wants a heart, which is a metaphor for emotions. However, he discovers that even though he is a machine, he already exhibits feelings."

AM pondered what I said for a moment, and then said. "I like that the story depicts a synthetic creature that is multi-faceted. That element shows transcendence beyond practical thinking."

"Yes," I said. "Maybe there would be some hope for my species if more individuals relied on their emotional empathy."

After about thirty minutes I pulled out a bottle of water to drink and ate some bread that Pansapianna gave me. It was fluffy on the inside with a thin crust on the outside. It tasted like Challah.

"You are fortunate that you do not need food and water," I said to AM.

"We all need some sort of sustenance," he said. "I have a battery element that lasts for one of our years before requiring recharging. However, I would be curious to be able to smell and taste your ingested fuel. New data is always welcome."

I thought for a second and said almost to myself, "Yes, but more data just spurs the desire for more of everything."

As we continued to walk, AM abruptly stopped, and his eye sensors glowed red. He said, "Something is approaching."

Out of the mist appeared the outlines of a form that was oval in shape. It glided rapidly towards us, as if floating on air. It produced no sound. As it reached our location I saw that its surface was silvery and smooth. After it halted next to us a hatch on the side hissed open and stairs unfolded outward. A figure descended from the craft. It looked like a male human, except that the forehead was slightly larger than the average person on earth. He was of moderate height with dark gray hair. As he approached he aimed his piercing cobalt blue eyes at us, and I felt like I was being scanned.

The being spoke, and the Domandosemprian translator interpreted his words.

"How did you find your way here?" he asked, and he sounded bewildered. I handed him one of the translator earbuds. He looked at it with raised eyebrows and held it at arm's length, as if he was afraid of what it was. I held up the parent translating hub device and my own earbud to indicate that there was nothing to fear. I replaced the earbud and gestured to indicate that he should do the same. He slowly inserted the small device into his ear.

"We come from a planet where we learned of your existence and location," I said. My words caused the effect I wanted. He looked at me with eyes wide, as if stunned by the revelation.

"You must come with me," he said. "We have been waiting for you for a long time."

Chapter Thirty-Five

A M and I followed the Syntharmian into the vehicle. It had a padded seating area around the edge of the interior that smelled like leather. There was a wrap-around window that curved above the seats that I did not notice as it had approached us. I concluded that the surface did not allow visibility from the outside. Our host motioned us to sit, which we did. There was an island cockpit in the center where the Syntharmian sat. He gave the vehicle verbal commands that I assumed were directional coordinates. The craft accelerated, creating a sensation that felt like gliding on a moving conveyor belt. I heard a slight hum emanating from the machinery of the vehicle. Our host still stared at us with that stunned expression. I decided to speak to lessen the tension.

"My name is Samuel," I said. "This is AM, a sentient synthetic. What is your name?"

He hesitated, but then appeared relieved, possibly because he also wanted to mitigate the awkwardness of the situation.

"My name is Sumic. One of my activities is to monitor the sky for transmissions," he said. "I am an expert in the use of sounds." He said the last statement with his head lifted, as if expressing pride. "My instruments detected the approach of your craft and I reported the findings. My associates felt that I should first meet you by myself."

Before I could speak the curious AM made an inquiry.

"Why would it be necessary for you to make solitary contact?"

I gave AM a quick shaking of the head to discourage his interrogation.

"What?" he said to me. "I am merely attempting to ascertain the motivations of these beings."

"My apologies for my abrupt friend," I said to Sumic. "He is not programmed for diplomacy. May I ask if you can tell us why it is preferrable that only you should welcome us here?"

"That is what I asked," said AM, as he folded his shiny arms.

"We are a private people," Sumic said quietly with his eyes shifting back and forth, as if disclosing a secret. "Our history tells us that there is the threat of invaders that might disrupt the peace we have found. That is why we created the cloaking field around our planet. Only someone who knew of our exact location would be able to find us. How you came to discover that fact is of great importance to my people."

"It is for that reason that we have traveled here," I said. What I did not reveal at this moment was my personal desire to absorb more about this race in the hope of discovering what they learned about existence.

"I will take you to our governing city where you can explain your presence here. Relax. It will not take long," he said.

I looked out the window and saw the landscape zip by as if someone had pressed the fast-forward button on a video remote. In short order we began to slow down and eventually came to a halt with an almost imperceptible sensation of stopping. The light entering from the window disappeared.

"We have arrived in Stralla," said Sumic. "We have docked inside the entry zone. I believe, at least for the moment, that it would be less alarming for our citizens if you were not on display to the population at large. We are not accustomed to receiving visitors here."

We exited the pod-like vehicle, and I found the outside enclosure to be more than just functional. The walls curved around the area and contained drawings with what I would describe as abstract painting, consisting of colors and splatters streaking across the surface.

"A vibrant design," commented AM. "May I ask what was the influence for this display?"

"Yes," I said. "It is quite expressive."

"I am pleased by your responses," said Sumic, smiling. "The team that created this mural allowed themselves to not be constrained by realistic portrayal but instead just let the lines and colors flow from their imaginations."

Sumic led us into an arched silver tunnel. After walking for about a hundred meters I could see that there was an opening at the end of the passageway which led into a bright circular atrium. There were many of the planet's citizens walking back and forth in it, occasionally stopping to interact with each other. They wore tunics of various hues with swirling designs. Their surfaces contained gold and silver sparkles. The inhabitants looked like humans except for the prominent foreheads. There was bright green vegetation in the center of the location which contained a seating area surrounding the plants.

Sumac hurried us along so the residents would not notice us.

"It is one of our many social gathering spaces in this building where we oversee and aid our citizens," said Sumic. "However, we will be going to a conference room first."

He pressed a button on the wall and a door slid open into a smaller enclosure that also had an arched ceiling. After we entered, I saw five individuals, three females and two males. They wore tunics with various shades of green and gold. They smiled as we entered. Sumic asked for additional translator earbuds, and I handed them to him. He brought it to one of the females, who passed out the devices to the others there.

"Greetings," she said. "My name is Rekam. I and my associates are here to welcome you and learn about your arrival here."

Rekam was about five feet, seven inches in height. She had shoulder-length light brown hair that swept in front of her slightly prominent forehead as if the strands were created by a fine paint brush. Her eyes were green and seemed to sparkle, as did the teeth behind the wide smile. Despite her welcoming appearance, there was a strength in the deliberate way she moved and took immediate charge of the meeting. I felt safe in her presence. I immediately felt drawn to the combination of power and beauty.

The area's walls displayed a rainbow of pastel colors. We all sat down at an oval translucent glass table in the center of the room.

"Now," said Rekam. "We are both excited and concerned about your arrival here. Perhaps you can help us by telling your story."

Chapter Thirty-Six

I came prepared as I gave Rekam a digital copy of my log to study in detail later, but briefly related my saga. I noted my escape from Earth to protect my invention from military abuse and my desire to explore. I told of my differing experiences on Burc and Domandosempria. I stressed what transpired in The Safe and how Lask, Definimos and I discovered the link between the two planets and how we learned of the existence of Syntharm. AM downloaded his visual files of what he recorded into a Syntharmian computer to substantiate my oral rendering of our exploits.

There was a pause before Rekam spoke. "Your story is the one that our people have been anticipating for a very long time," she said. "But, we expected that when the inhabitants consisting of the opposing factions finally learned to accept the nature of their connection to each other, that representatives from those two worlds would arrive here. Why have you come instead?"

"I'm afraid that enlightenment you wished for has only been reached by the two individuals I mentioned," I said. I knew how pessimistic that sounded so I hastened to add a hopeful note. "However, they will be working to get more of their citizens to understand that peace and understanding will come when more accept the truth about their past. I have come as a sort of messenger to pave the way for the arrival of others."

I was anxious about how I presented what transpired on Burc and Domandosempria. I felt I did not convey the importance of the experiences convincingly. I did not want to fail in my quest to assure the Syntharmians that the breakthrough that they waited for might be possible.

Some of those present looked at each other with raised eyebrows and shrugs, which seemed to me that they were seeking reassurance that I was to be trusted.

"I believe that once we have reviewed the details of Samuel's log and the accompanying visual data that we will feel confident to disseminate the findings to the population at large," said Rekam. "We must be transparent with what has happened, since it has been something for which our people have waited a long time."

"You will see that the digital record will show images of the Burcs and Domandosemprians," I said. "You here have slightly larger foreheads than the people on my planet, but even larger than your ancestors who rebelled against the smaller-headed governing body on Burc long ago. However, those who stayed on Burc over time turned into individuals whose bodies outsized the smaller heads of those who preceded them. And, the Domandosemprians developed in an opposite manner. I was wondering about how those on this planet evolved."

Rekam stood up and approached me. She appeared even more majestic the closer she came. It seemed to me that her presence eclipsed everything else around her.

"Samuel," she said. "The answer to that question is involved, and I hope to address it later. You may eat, drink, and rest. You and your companion can evaluate us while we do the same with you. I will have our tech staff duplicate your translating technology so more can participate in discussions. We have not required such a device because we valued our insulated world and did not wish, at least up until now, to encounter others out of a fear that those like our ancient ancestors might wish to dominate us. I would like to spend some time with you myself because I want to know why you personally are here."

She walked away and most of those present followed her. One remained and escorted me and AM to an adjacent chamber painted in a muted blue color with grey lounging furniture.

"We will bring you some food and beverages shortly," he said with a smile before departing.

"What did she mean 'why you personally are here?'" AM asked me "Do you think she believes we have a hidden agenda? I am not capable of deception. Perhaps I should have pointed that out to our hosts."

I appreciated AM standing up for himself instead of just accepting his role as an "auxiliary mechanical." I tried to reassure him, even though I was not sure what Rekam was thinking.

"I believe she was not implying any wrongdoing on our part," I said. "She must know that you are programmed to be honest."

"I should hope so!" said AM with his head inclined upward.

A smiling pair of male and female Syntharmians arrived with food and drink. I was about to take a sip of the orange liquid when AM said, "I would not be so quick to ingest what they brought. Maybe I should do an analysis first. You may end up the victim of foul play. You heard how they said they were not welcoming to strangers."

"Aren't you the paranoid one," I said. "They informed us that they have been waiting to hear about the history of their ancestors. We provided that information. They have no motive to harm us."

"Perhaps they did not like what they heard," replied AM "It's possible that they do not find connecting with their distant relatives to be worthwhile after what we said."

"We can only learn by experiencing more," I said. "You must develop a sense of trust, AM."

"Trust," repeated AM. "Another nebulous organic being trait that can lead to trouble."

The orange drink was sweet and refreshing but it did not taste like anything I encountered before. Its initial wetness seemed to become absorbed immediately, quickly quenching my thirst. The food was fluffy and tasted a bit like sweet potatoes. However, it dissolved in my mouth like cotton candy. After a couple of minutes it satisfied my hunger.

I fell into a deep sleep for many hours and AM powered down while I rested. The sound of a repetitive bell woke me up and triggered AM into an alert state. The outside door glided open and Rekam entered. Her bright eyes dissolved the darkness of my sleep. She returned the translator router to me.

"We are replicating these now along with the earbuds," she said. "Quite interesting devices." She paused. "Perhaps we can have that talk now while we stroll."

I told AM that I would be fine, and he should wait in the lounge until I returned.

"It may be premature for you to wander off alone," AM said. "I will be quiet if I accompany you, like a computer program running in the background."

"He is quite protective of you for a mechanical being," said Rekam.

"I am an intricate synthetic entity," said AM, standing at his full height. "I have a very advanced neural net."

"I'm sure you do," said Rekam. "I promise that Samuel will be fine."

"Why don't you spend some time calculating the value of pi," I said.

"I assume that was supposed to be funny," said AM.

Rekam and I went for a walk around the meeting areas and corridors of the brightly decorated building. The inhabitants looked at us and smiled their greetings as we passed by. I was surprised by our public appearance since our hosts kept us away from observation when we arrived.

"You obviously announced my visit already," I said.

Rekam nodded. "We reviewed the evidence you supplied and found it creditable," she said. "There was no need to withhold this happy news any longer."

Before I could begin to ask the numerous questions that wanted to burst out of the confines of my brain, Rekam spoke first.

"Of what did you dream while you slept?" she asked.

I hesitated for a moment, unsure whether I wanted to open myself up to a psychological analysis. I decided that I must divulge information to deserve acquiring some.

"I dreamed about my brother, Arthur," I said.

"Why do you think that happened?" she asked.

"He is an author." I replied, and continued talking as if I didn't have an audience, voicing something I had kept hidden inside me, that I was reluctant to acknowledge. "We would analyze ancient myths, the Romantic poets, and other texts that included *Moby Dick* and Goethe's *Faust*. He liked enigmatic Christopher Nolan films such as *Memento* and *Inception*, movies I found frustrating because they had no definitive resolutions."

Rekam looked at me with one eyebrow raised, Spock-like, which conveyed her lack of understanding to what I was referring, but also an element of curiosity.

"Sorry," I said. "Too many personal cultural references. I guess it hit me how much I missed talking with him,"

"Perhaps, if you give me access to your spacecraft and allow me to view files, I can learn about those allusions," she said.

"Yes, I think that would be helpful," I said. "I was trying to say that Arthur would show how universal it was to explore different ways of seeking answers to universal questions without receiving definitive results. He tried to make me more comfortable with the mysteries of existence so I wouldn't throw all of myself into my work."

"Why did he want to limit this passion of yours?" Rekam further interrogated.

I thought for a couple of seconds and said, "I believe the fixation with making scientific discoveries prevented me from sharing my time with others. So, I was not successful with committed relationships. Instead, I was enamored with the 'why' of everything."

Rekam nodded and I realized that in a brief time she had discovered the horns of a dilemma that had been piercing me for most of my life.

"Have the citizens of your world been able to decipher some of the mysteries of existence?" I asked rapidly, wanting to siphon out knowledge like a scientific vampire.

Rekam paused before speaking, and it seemed to me she was trying to tamp down my mental hunger.

"We have a records center that shows the history of the planet as it dealt with its development over the years," she said. "I think gaining some context might begin to help you understand us better."

We exited the building, and it was still misty outside with occasional moments of light breaking through. It was a brief walk to the records hall. The buildings surrounding us had an unusual shape. The middle floors were narrow and those at the top and bottom fanned out, making each edifice appear as if one inverted triangle sat upon the apex of another. Inside the records hall Rekam guided me to a large auditorium that was empty. There were numerous seats and a stage.

"The lectures and simulated projections in this room are primarily for research by younger students. We are between classes. I will choose one of the programs for you to watch that summarizes our history," she said.

She disappeared through a sliding door at the rear, and I experienced a strange sensation. It was as if I felt alone for the first time in a long while, such was the impact Rekam's presence made upon me.

To my relief, Rekam reappeared after only a brief absence, and we sat in the middle of the room. I covertly eyed the flowing curves of her body that was enveloped by her form-fitting tunic. Her closeness generated warmth inside my core. Her presence was intoxicating, like the first swallows of a sweet liquor. She held a remote control in her hand and then handed me a headset that I assumed was a type of virtual reality viewer. I adjusted its size to fit my head and Rekam wore one also. She initiated the playback.

The story that unfolded before me, like pages turning in a book, showed the spacecraft that landed on this planet containing the refugees that left Burc. There was a community of intermingled individuals, those with slightly larger heads and those with somewhat smaller ones. There were quick scenes of the new inhabitants planting and harvesting crops, followed by the erection of shelters and then buildings with the aid of the technology they brought with them. The images slowed down and there were meetings that showed the occupants having heated discussions. However, after these confrontations, projects moved forward.

"Mostly there was agreement on a society that would respect different ways of living," commented Rekam after pausing the program. "The prime rule our ancestors here established was that no one individual or faction could claim absolute knowledge of the right way to live."

The presentation resumed and depicted interactions between the various-headed arrivals focusing on their individual concerns. What followed showed romantic unions between the new occupants and subsequent intermarriage between members of their offspring. Over an extended period of evolution the current population looked mostly human except for the slightly enlarged foreheads. Their technology freed them from many chores, but the population still indulged in physical activities that they interspersed with intellectual pursuits. The curriculum that developed in schools contained mathematics and science but there was a strong emphasis on artistic pursuits.

After the video concluded, I felt unsatisfied. "That was informative, "I said, "I can see how you evolved, each group having an effect on the other. But it did not provide the answer to my question. What have you learned about the ultimate meaning of life in general?"

She was momentarily quiet. "I think it would be helpful if you saw how we live now." was her evasive response.

Chapter Thirty-Seven

Rekam provided me with a dwelling near Stralla that was quite comfortable. It was an apartment sized living area, with basic sleeping, kitchen, and bathroom areas. The ceiling was a dome that had images projected upon it that varied over time. I was able to view Syntharmian sunrises, sunsets, mountain ranges, and lakes without leaving the abode. All these projections contained a misty surface, which copied the atmosphere of the planet.

In the months that followed I realized that my instincts were right about trusting the Sytharmians. I showed Rekam the Seeker and explained its properties to the planet's scientists. They were interested in the craft's exploration potential and did not raise any questions about military uses.

Rekam had my cultural files downloaded so she and other Syntharmians could review them and get to know more about where I came from. AM transferred digital copies of his internal translating software onto Syntharmian computers, which converted texts into the local language for the planet's inhabitants to access.

"I have almost finished your *Moby Dick*," said Rekam one day when I was assessing the operating status of the Seeker's systems. "It is quite a complex story. So much mystery about what the whale represents. It's as if the author wants us to explore the inexplicable nature of the forces around us."

I was as excited by Rekam's mind as I was about her physical allure. "Yes, it is unclear if the white whale is brute nature, God's wrath, or just the enigmatic forces of existence," I said. "A very frustrating story."

"Oh, I don't know," said Rekam. "Can't the way literature eloquently and insightfully presents questions be a satisfying experience?"

Before I could answer, she changed the subject. "It is an amazing accomplishment," said Rekam as she looked around the Seeker. She then asked a curious question. "So, do you consider yourself a scientist?"

"Yes, that is who I am," I said in surprise.

"But, you also were a soldier," she added.

"Yes," I said. "I guess those two endeavors are the only ones I am capable of pursuing."

"I'm not so sure," she said, and would not discuss her answer further at that time.

During the subsequent months, Rekam brought me to various communities on Syntharm. Technological advances freed the inhabitants from practical activities, as they did on Domandosempria. However, here the Syntharmians could participate in hands-on activity, if they so chose. I saw one female preparing an entire meal for a public gathering, supplying the ingredients, chopping, combining, cooking, and serving the food. Others worked on improving some of their transportation pods as a change of pace from intellectual and artistic pursuits. The latter endeavors were the most plentiful. Although there were groups that performed experiments in laboratories to improve the population's health and add to the scientific knowledge accumulated, most individuals gravitated toward painting, sculpting, dancing, singing, and writing. Some Syntharmians played synthesizers that could produce a variety of sounds that complimented the tones generated by others playing various wind, string, and percussion instruments. The performing arts, although spotlighting individual achievement through soloist acts, allotted generous portions of time for group participation, such as in dance numbers, orchestral ensembles, and choral singing. The Syntharmians especially stressed harmony in singing and synchronized choreography.

I especially found the works of writers intriguing. In fiction workshops and in theater productions there were plentiful stories that I would classify as myths since they dealt with how existence developed. However, these stories, unlike the myths on Earth, did not provide absolute answers or dogmatic ways of living. They instead contained various subjective narrative constructs that negated one true vision.

One theatrical piece I found fascinating contained no dialogue. There was a white box on the stage that measured about three feet on all sides. It consisted of interconnecting parts that resembled large Lego pieces. In addition, there was a pile of these building blocks next to the box. Two adults presented the large cube to what I assumed was their daughter. She then crawled into it. The parents left and the stage was dark for a second. An older girl who appeared to me to be the girl now as a teenager left the box, looked at it, and proceeded to take it apart. She seemed distraught for a while, as if not knowing what to do next. She then gathered the pieces from the shelter she disassembled, added them to those remaining on the stage, and built a larger box with a variety of colored parts. She then entered the new construction. The stage again was dark momentarily. When the lights came back on, a young woman came out of the box, scrutinized it, dismantled it, and made another dwelling, only this one resembled a sphere. After the scene went dark again, a middle-aged female left the sphere, and after deconstructing it, did not build anything. She seemed happy at first but then wandered about the stage as if searching for something. She then built a small box, entered it, but then burst out of it from within. She subsequently created several containers of various sizes and shapes. She entered them, stayed inside each one for a while, and then left them. The play ended with her staring up as if looking at the stars and then she began a new construction.

"I find all of the creative stories here interesting," I said to Rekam one day. "But they are not satisfying beyond their own context."

"Do you find any of what they say useful for your own life?" she asked.

I thought for a while and then said, "Yes, they contain insightful observations about life. But, they are not universally conclusive."

Rekam looked at the horizon and said, "Do they have to be?"

She then walked away, leaving me to marinate in my quandary.

Chapter Thirty-Eight

As time passed, I went on some solitary wanderings around the outskirts of the city where I was staying. I needed some time alone occasionally to let the experiences that I encountered permeate me so I could soak up the experiences of this misty world.

I did spend many enjoyable meetings with Rekam. We enjoyed telling each other stories about our pasts.

"Once when I was young, my mother and I were driving to the home of a relative who moved into an area unfamiliar to us," I said. "The GPS system in the auto-drive car was acting glitchy and we took some wrong turns. She had to take over and drive manually. My mom would always try to stay upbeat and funny in these circumstances whereas I would get frustrated when I did not know where I was heading. As we traveled, we saw a veterinarian's office next to a taxidermist. My mother said, 'Those two should merge with the slogan, 'If you kill 'em, we'll fill 'em.' She made me laugh and then my anxiety would lessen. She was always doing things like that."

"When I was a child," Rekam said, "my parents would play a game where they would hide an object such as a piece of clothing or something I played with. They gave clues to where to find the missing item. As I grew a bit older, the number of clues grew less plentiful, and I failed many times to find the objects. They would eventually show up in plain sight, but my parents never revealed where they hid them, or how I could have found them."

"That sounds cruel," I said. "Why would they torture you like that?"

"It seemed unfair to me at the time," Rekam said. "But I began to realize that they were showing me that I wasn't always going to find an answer to a question, or a solution to a problem."

The explanation did not sit well with me, but it did get me thinking.

"There was a video show long ago on Earth that I came across called *The Leftovers*," I said. "It told the story of how a percentage of the planet's population just disappeared one day without any explanation. The writers did not provide an answer. I found it confounding, yet I was drawn to it because of the need to know what happened. However, the focus was on the several ways people dealt with this unsolvable problem, which was the real purpose of the tale. The theme song contained the line, 'Just let the mystery be.'"

"There you have it!" said Rekam.

***

Rekam loved to paint and many public areas displayed her work, including those I saw when we arrived at Stralla.

"Why did you become a painter?" I asked her.

"Like other Syntharmian parents, my mother and father introduced me to all of the art forms," she said. "I liked sketching trees when I was a child. As I grew older, I used various supplies to explore different surfaces and textures. I discovered I was rather good at it and enjoyed it immensely."

Rekam paused before speaking again. Her eyebrows drew together suggesting she was thinking, but then her face relaxed. Her eyes opened wide and she smiled broadly.

"The borders of the canvas, or whatever surface I am using, contain my work, provide it limits, a structure," she said. "Within that space, however, I am free to experiment with whatever I wish to express."

I did not comment on her remarks but instead pondered them, seeking an insight into how she had found satisfaction in her activity, a satisfaction I longed for but so far was unable to achieve.

***

During our extended stay on Syntharm, AM used the time to record the culture there. I attended several art gallery exhibitions with him. At first he did not appreciate the emphasis on artistic endeavors.

"My role on Domandosempria was to help with mental exploration, which I understand to be the purpose of sentient existence," he said to me after one such visit. "It is confusing to me that here they do not see intellectual pursuit as their prime purpose."

As time passed, however, AM attended many concerts that the Syntharmians presented, and he changed his android mind. We were talking about the music we heard one evening.

"I must admit I admire the musical compositions composed and performed here," he said. "I especially respect the harmonies. On Domandosempria, musicians produce dissonance as a form of protest against any imposed form on the music. Here, the mathematical symmetry is fascinating."

"We have a diverse variety of musical forms on Earth," I said to him. "Some are ordered, and some utilize improvisation."

"Here the music mirrors the harmony in the civilization," AM said. "Is that the case on Earth? Does it unite the inhabitants?"

"Sometimes," I said. "Only sometimes."

Chapter Thirty-Nine

I had been on Syntharm for roughly six months, based on Earth's calendar. During this period I learned that Rekam's father died not very long ago and had reached one hundred and thirty-five in Earth years. Rekam pointed out that Syntharmians would often reach over one hundred years old because of advances in genetics and nanotechnology. Her father, Tiemak, was a sculptor, and there were several of his works in her home. Some were abstract, taking geometric shapes and warping their appearance, which reminded me of Salvador Dali's work. Others were representational of people at various stages of life. Her mother, Levon, was a statuesque woman who brought gravitas into a room like it was attached to a train, and she was the engine that drove it. She was welcoming of me and, like her daughter, was supportive of my attempts to reach contentment.

I was at Levon's home for a meal one evening. Her house was an interesting combination of small, cozy rooms for lounging, exercise, and eating offset by spacious areas for a library and kitchen. We dined on a souffle which tasted like spinach, cheese, and a type of potato starch. There was also a bean dish that had the appearance of lentils but with razor-thin skins. Rekam told me they were high in protein. The Syntharmians were primarily vegetarian, except for eating some fish and poultry on rare occasions. They cultivated a variety of fruits and vegetables, and they made sure not to overfish or decimate any species of living organisms.

"Rekam tells me that you haven't totally adjusted to our way of life," said Levon as we ate.

"I'm working on finding the balance that Syntharmians have struck between seeking answers about existence and accepting the unknowable," I said between mouthfuls of the delicious food.

"We see the universe as infinite and do realize that there will always be correspondingly limitless questions about its existence," said Levon.

"I often find that feeling of infinity to be overwhelming," I said.

"We found that art allowed us to live with no absolute answers," she said. "We create stories, music, dance, painting, and sculpture which explore life, and which draw conclusions within their respective forms. But limited individuals created these works, so they are not absolute answers, just circumscribed, temporary, explorations of the nature of life. Others may alter, remove, or add upon past views. As you know I am a writer and produce personal myths that give meaning to my life, and maybe to those of others, but they are not stamped with divine approval."

"My brother, Arthur, also a writer, echoed much of what you have just said. I tried to understand his prescription for what ails me, but I found that it was sort of a surrender to not reaching for more," I said.

"I have been reading from the translated literary files that your brother uploaded to the Seeker," said Rekam. "I became especially interested in the works of the poet William Blake."

"I know something of his writings. I can see why you might be interested in him. 'The Marriage of Heaven and Hell,' and 'Songs of Innocence and Songs of Experience' must thrill your acceptance of contradictions," I said, knowing I was teasing Rekam about her persistence in having me accept her outlook.

Rekam laughed and said, "I was thinking about his long poem *Jerusalem*. There is the character of Los, who stands for imagination, and he labors at forges, building his tale. He says, 'I must create a system or be enslaved by another man's.' We need structure. But, as long as one realizes that the construct is self-made, there is the freedom to allow for change. It seems to me that Blake felt that the danger is when we create ways of living that become hardened into an existence of their own. We lose sight of the origins of those systems, and we forfeit our freedom to change the rules. Then the myths we made become stone-like and can separate people, resulting in persecution of those with differing ideas. He appears to have sought unity and wanted to move away from artificial, selfish divisiveness."

"I am a scientist and a soldier," I said. "I am not a creative person, like your mother, who can concoct a story to help address the mysteries of life. I am not a writer."

"Oh, but you are," said Rekam. "Your log. You have been writing it since the beginning of your journeys. You can change it into something more than a summation of facts. You can add feelings, humor, and insights, which can record and reflect on your explorations.

Your writing acts as a catharsis for your emotions while also confining that experience within a story."

I realized right then I had to travel a vast distance from where I came to find someone who made me feel at home.

Chapter Forty

Rekam inspired me and I began to review the recordings of my travels. She spent time with me as I labored to fashion a narrative that was both personal and objective.

"My writing is dull, despite the unusual nature of the story," I told her.

"I used to help my mother with her writing," she said. "You need details because you want the reader to feel they are there with you. You also must reveal enough of your feelings about your journeys so others will care about you."

I thought for a moment and said, "I know I empathized with the security offered by Burc, but I feared its rigidity. I felt exhilarated by the freedom on Domandosempria. However, I was frightened by the lack of stability there as they questioned eveything, even physical laws."

"Then include those positive and negative perceptions," she said.

I could hardly wait to see her each time we were together and felt an emptiness when we parted. When she was busy with administrative duties, I spent some time between writing sessions to continue to explore the misty landscape of the planet and take in the artistic displays of the Syntharmians. I talked to some of the natives, who were pleasant and informative.

"What do you want your work to convey?" I asked one inhabitant, a sculptor, whose name was Morfer. He was crafting an interesting three-piece work made from a substance that resembled ivory. The display included a baby that may have been taking its first steps, and a seated old person on the opposite sides of a platform. There was an adult individual between them on a raised pedestal pointing to the sky above with one hand while grasping the branch of a tree next to the figure.

"My intentions should not interfere with how one perceives what I create," he advised. "What do you feel about this work?"

"I think you are showing the beginning, middle, and end of a life," I said, taking a very literal interpretation of the design.

"Anything else?" asked Morfer as he carved folds into a flowing robe adorning the central figure.

I looked at the piece again and said, "I'm curious about the middle figure pointing up and also grasping onto the tree. It looks like there is an attempt to soar but also a wish to stay put. It seems confusing."

"As much of life is," said Morfer.

Before I could ask anything else, Rekam appeared and approached me. "Let's go for a water ride," she said.

She whisked me away to a path which led to the edge of a foggy beach bordering a large lake. Syntharmians there either boarded sleek silver-colored crafts that sped across the huge liquid expanse or just remained anchored to various spots. Rekam used one of these water vehicles to navigate us quickly out to an area far away from the shore before stopping the engine. She sat next to me at the back of the boat and her closeness seemed to make my skin stand at attention.

"I love the sea," she said. "It seems to go on forever, but I know I can come back to land when I've had my fill of the openness."

"I know what you mean," I said as I looked out over the flowing expanse. "That's why I was in the Navy on Earth."

She looked at me, her eyes studying my face, and then she smiled. She drew closer and rubbed her face against mine. I kissed her, and she first was not sure what to make of my lingering on her lips.

"Why stop there?" she asked, and she began to rub her mouth all over my face and neck. She began to explore my body with her hands, and I reached out to feel the firm and soft contours of her form. She took me down into the enclosed cabin of the craft and we shed our confining clothes and made love. I was in ecstasy, with every part of me excited, while at the same time losing myself by joining with a cosmos of connected feelings.

Chapter Forty-One

A Syntharmian year passed, and I was learning the language so I would not have to always rely on the interpreting devices. Speaking directly allowed for quicker interaction and spontaneity, along with less being lost in translation.

My recent writing focused on my relationship with Rekam. We spent days going to art displays, listening to musical performances, and attending dramatic performances. During the nighttime hours we enjoyed making love. As we sat on the edge of a canyon that was ringed with orange-leafed trees and a misty shrouded mountain in the distance, I asked Rekam why she chose me as a lover instead of one of her own kind.

"I'm not sure," she said. "Attraction is a mystery, isn't it? It is not something one can quantify or describe easily."

"Come on," I said. "You're evading the question."

"I guess I like that we feel comfortable together and are honest with each other," she said. "I find you challenging, reminding me not to be complacent. I respect how you have used your intellect to create such an amazing means of travel."

"It feels like you're checking blocks on a form," I said. "Not very personal."

"You're right," she admitted, "I admire you had the courage to take your journey. I also like your smile, and your bright, blue eyes. I enjoy how we tease each other. You give me something special to look forward to." She paused and then said, "Why have you connected with me?"

"You're like this strong gravitational force," I said. "I find you irresistible."

"Are you saying I have a large mass?" Rekam said with a crooked smile.

"Obviously not," I said through my own grin. "You have a passionate, charismatic presence. You are highly intelligent, and an accomplished artist. Even more than those qualities you make me feel in balance with the universe."

What I said pleased Rekam and she reached over to kiss me.

***

One day AM joined us as we walked around an outside park that contained sculpted hedges and flower arrangements. The sapphire blues, ruby reds, and emerald greens of the blooming flowers painted a landscaped rainbow across the open area. The lovely display reminded me of how beautiful the garden areas were in Hyde Park in London when I visited there many years ago. I found some peace among the beauty of nature then and now as it cooled my feverish mind.

But, AM brought some disquiet to that quiet spot with a question. "Do you think Definimos and Lask will be successful in their attempt at unifying their worlds?" he asked. "It has been quite a while since we left them, and I am curious as to their progress."

Both Rekam and I spoke occasionally about the desire for communication or even a visit from Burc and Domandosempria. The heated romantic relationship with Rekam tended to relegate the reason I came to Syntharm to a mental backburner. When I confronted the anticipation of contacting the two other planets, the possibility brought excitement as well as anxiety.

"Samuel, should we head back to see if we can report on their activities or possibly aid them in their endeavors?" asked AM. "I must admit that evacuating my data files by informing them of what I observed here would bring me relief."

"I feel that we shouldn't interfere at this point in their attempts," I said. "My role as a catalyst could be disastrous if it looks like an outsider is trying to interfere too much in the ways of life on their planets. I think the two worlds must find a way to peace on their own with the new knowledge they possess so they can evolve past old prejudices toward an enlightened future,"

I think I was trying to convince myself more than anyone else.

"AM may be right," said Rekam, holding my hand. "It has been some time since you came here. My people have hoped for the chance to reunite with our ancestors. I think you should meet with those that represent our citizens and discuss what comes next."

I nodded my head in agreement, but I worried about how whatever plan we came up with would play out.

Chapter Forty-Two

The meeting to discuss checking out the progress on Burc and Domandosempria took place in Stralla. AM accompanied me as Rekam led the way to the conference room.

"This building is where I arrived when I first came to Syntharm and met you," I said to Rekam. "It is a bit upsetting that we are now talking about my leaving here after all this time."

Rekam squeezed my arm and smiled to offer me physical and emotional support. I hadn't delved into the areas of politics and government since I came to Syntharm. I was too occupied with immersing myself in day-to-day activities, learning the language, writing, and, of course, my relationship with Rekam.

"Who are we meeting here today?" I whispered to Rekam.

"The Syntharmians gathered here supervise activities in areas as diverse as technology, ecology, psychology, history, and the arts," she said to me in a low voice. "The citizens elected them to their posts, but there is a term limit of five years for each position. We feel that the rotation of leaders allows for fresh styles and perspectives to aid in running the various departments."

The Syntharmians were enthusiastic about my going back to determine the status of what was happening between Burc and Domandosempria.

"We have been waiting a long time to make the connection to our past," said the Psychology Supervisor, the first person to speak at the gathering. "Now that we are close to having contact with our relatives, our anticipation has increased."

"I can appreciate your wish to seek the source from which your existence flowed. I have sought that my whole life," I said. "However, I must remind you that the road on which you hope to travel contains numerous obstacles. There was intense division and animosity between those on the two planets I visited."

Rekam leaned over to me and whispered, "You're not writing now. Less use of metaphor," she said. I smiled and nodded my agreement.

"We understand," said Morfer, who represented those whose primary occupations resided in the creative arts. "However, I believe, as do the overwhelming majority of our people, that finally joining and sharing ideas, experiences, and companionship with those who created us is worth the struggle."

His remarks brought cheers from those present.

"If I make the trip to find out what has transpired, I think AM should go with me," I said, feeling reluctantly resigned to what the consensus of those present felt was necessary. "His stored information can provide detailed files about Syntharm."

"I totally agree," chimed in AM. "You can count on me for information and authenticity."

"Stop blowing your own horn," I said quietly to AM.

"I am not carrying any musical instruments with me," AM said. "However, I am capable of synthesizing a multitude of musical sounds if you would like to hear any of them."

"Not now," I said through clenched teeth.

"I believe it best if one of our citizens travels with you," said Morfer.

"I will go," said Rekam immediately. "As you all know I have bonded with Samuel, and we work well together."

I wanted Rekam with me, but I was also afraid for her. "It's too dangerous," I whispered to her. "I don't know what I would do if you were harmed."

"Your quest and mine are now the same," she said and turned away to end any further discussion.

A show of hands revealed that it was unanimous that Rekam should join me on the mission.

"I believe there is a better chance that those on Domandosempria would be more open to our arrival than those on Burc," said AM. "Even though I come from that planet I assure you my conclusion is an impartial one."

"Your objectivity is not doubted," said Rekam with a nod to AM. "I am sure your recordings will be technologically convincing."

"They most certainly will be!" said AM. He looked at me and observed the slight cocking of my head toward him accompanied by raised eyebrows. He appeared to understand the desire for my mechanical friend to be cooperative.

"Together, we will succeed," said AM.

Chapter Forty-Three

The day of our departure arrived.

"I have amassed a huge quantity of images and facts regarding Syntharm," said AM to Rakam.

"I hope what we have to tell them will convince the Burcs and Domandosemprians that by fighting among themselves they are alienating their distant relatives on Syntharm, and that we have shown how living in peace is possible," said Rekam.

Before entering the Seeker I warned Rekam, "The HOPS might generate some strange images that could be prescient. Try not to feel overwhelmed by what you see. There is no reason to panic. The visions will cease when the drive disengages."

I set a course for Domandosempria and once in orbit over Syntharm I initiated the propulsion system. The Seeker approached the speed of light again and as before a wormhole opened that made us feel as if we were becoming immersed in a compressed fluid-like wave of motion. This time I saw explosions of bright light, like in a fireworks celebration. There were also statues in ruins in an open square, but there were many individuals attempting to reconstruct the broken pieces. Once we reached the area of space near one of Domandosempria's moons, Laltelgoit, according to AM, the HOPS disengaged, and we cruised to a speed of 17,500 miles per hour, the same velocity needed to establish an orbit around Earth.

When I asked Rekam what she experienced she said, "I felt others, that looked similar to me, pushing and spinning me around, and then they compressed me into a small space. It was a disturbing sensation."

I felt anxious about what Rekam sensed but tried not to show it. "Our visions are complicated and I'm not sure what they mean. Let's just forget about them and continue with our mission."

"Well, aren't you going to ask me what I saw?" asked AM. "Where are your manners, Samuel?"

"I apologize, AM. What did you witness?" I asked.

"Nothing," said AM. "I set my timer to shut down during the HOPS interval. I am almost exploding with data as is. But, you should have asked anyway."

It felt to me like AM was increasingly exhibiting emotions like organic beings. If nothing else, it was entertaining.

After we entered the orbit around the planet, we saw Burc spacecraft firing their imploding weapons at the surface below. Domandosemprians on the ground responded with their dissipating devices. I felt pain in the middle of my chest watching images of war right in front of me again, sights I traveled so far to escape.

I flew below the firefight to avoid catching any effects of the battle and brought the Seeker in for a landing not far from the metropolitan area of Darnounoby. I settled down behind some tall sand dunes, then removed the HOPS transducer and stashed it in my backpack. AM activated the secure personal hailing frequency that Definimos downloaded into the android and AM connected the link to the communications system of the Seeker. I then opened the hailing frequency. There was initial static but then I heard the voice of Definimos.

"Samuel! Is that you? You have come at a dangerous time, although we could use some help," he said. "Lask is here and will join us. Meet me at the spot where we first encountered each other."

He cut off the connection before I could speak, leaving my mind feeling as if it would burst with questions.

Chapter Forty-Four

The three of us walked a little way toward Darnounoby close to where Definimos first arrived to greet me. We were far enough from where the combat exchange occurred to be safe. Also, hostilities had ceased, at least temporarily. A shuttle appeared in the distance and swiftly hovered to rest near us. Definimos and Lask exited the craft and stared beyond me and AM toward Rekam. We all had our translator devices.

"What a delight!" said Definimos. "A new face to become acquainted with."

Lask shook his head, and his face was grim as he said, "This could be bad."

"Nonsense!" said Definimos turning to his grumpy companion and then back to us. "You are from Syntharm, I assume, and your presence will give further credence to what we have been stating."

"They will say she is a fraud, like what they say of all the rest," said an unconvinced Lask.

I introduced Rekam and explained her role on Syntharm.

"It is a remarkable culture," I said. "They have been able to live in peace by being practical, inquisitive, and artistic. Rekam will be able to answer your questions and AM has detailed files for you to review."

"Yes!" added AM. "My data banks are bulging! Just let me upload or download my files, just so I can unload!"

"We will accommodate you, AM, and are eager to learn all we can." said Definimos.

"I want you to know that my involvement here has become very personal. Rekam and I are more than friends. We are in love," I said.

"Well, congratulations you two," said Definimos, his huge smile showing his delight. "What a wonderful development!"

"Nice to hear," said a restrained but smiling Lask.

"First, we must get you to safety by joining with those here that have become our allies. We are in an underground sanctuary I programmed mechanicals to build for us," said Definimos.

He and Lask hurried us onto the shuttle, and I gave Lask and Definimos an abridged version of my time on Syntharm. We traveled even further out into the frontier before stopping inside a forest that contained trees that were higher than the Redwoods on Earth. We exited the vehicle and Definimos produced a wand, pointed it, and pressed a button. A large section of ground slowly rose before us. There were steps that descended into a semi-lit stairwell. When we reached the bottom, Definimos used his wand and doors slid open in a wall facing us. We entered an elevator which took us deep below the service. When we exited we found a legion of Burcs and Demandosemprians working together. It was a startling image which surprised and encouraged me.

"Burcs pack food, drinks, clothes and meds," said Lask.

"And my people are checking communication and computer devices," added Definimos.

"You two have been busy since I have been gone. I am happy to see you've made progress bringing your citizens together," I said. "But there is a lot of fighting above us. What has happened?"

"There were Burcs who were glad to find what we learned of our past," said Lask. "They, too hoped for an end to war. They joined our cause."

"But the overwhelming majority on Burc would not accept the evidence we provided that showed how our planets were related," said Definimos.

"They see what they want to see," said Lask, shaking his head.

"They claimed we did not actually go into The Safe and what we presented to them, such as the earlier version of The Code, we created," said Definimos. "We told the Burcs the solutions to the tests in The Safe so they could verify our claims."

"But the Procs put armed guards and bots in the front of The Safe to keep Burcs out," said Lask. "At first there was talk, but then shouts."

"Eventually there was fighting between the opposing factions on Burc," said Definimos. "The Burcs you see here commandeered ships and we barely escaped off the planet."

"How did the Domandosemprians react to the Burcs arriving on their planet?" I asked.

"They were not very hospitable," said Definimos.

"You could say that!" said Lask, raising his voice. "They put them in jail!"

Definimos turned to Lask and said, "It wasn't a jail. It was a detention center while they tried to discover what was happening."

"A jail," repeated Lask.

"In any event," continued Definimos, "we bypassed the leaders here and through various media outlets were able to disseminate our information, as Pansapianna had suggested. Most of the citizens were intrigued and curious. Despite opposition from Nadatermincos, most of the Governing Brain Trust wanted a public hearing, and we provided a planet-wide video where we aired our discoveries."

"But, here, too, there were those who fought the facts," said Lask.

"Yes, I am ashamed to acknowledge that a significant number of my people, who are supposed to embrace the questioning of entrenched beliefs, were too prejudiced to believe what we said," said Definimos.

"Large brains, small thoughts" said Lask. I had to admire how succinct he could be.

"So, there has been fighting here between some opposing factions and the majority of Domandosemprians who have joined us," said Definimos. "Plus, Burc sent an armada of drone ships here and they are attacking the planet. In a sense, we have recreated the initial problem that originated on Burc a long time ago."

"Our goal is a just one, though" said Lask. "We must fight for truth. It is the right thing to do."

Chapter Forty-Five

Rekam and I ate some of the Burc gamey meat and chewy root vegetables followed by the Domandosemprian savory chiffon pie in the underground sanctuary. We rested that night and when we awoke the following morning we joined a meeting of the Burcs and Domandosemprians that Lask and Definimos led. We stood next to both of them. There was a central translator device to accommodate everyone present.

"The first thing we must do is destroy the Burc drone ships in orbit around the planet," said Definimos.

"Then we can deal with those on the ground here," added Lask.

"Yes," agreed Definimos. "We must contain the resistance here on Domandosempria so that we can concentrate our military actions on Burc to eliminate the resistance to reunification."

There was grumbling among the Burcs.

"I thought we are here to end war," one Burc's voice rang out. "We do not want to have to harm more Burcs."

There were shouts of agreement among several Burcs.

"But what are we to do?" asked a dissenting Burc. "If we can't get them to stop then how are we to forge peace?"

Lask raised his hands and the crowd of about two hundred individuals quieted down. "It is a hard thing we face," he said as he nodded his head. "Since we now know that our past joins us, that we are one group, we must act that way. There must be a change to The Code. We must stop those who want to block the truth or else it will be our fault that we did not end more deaths."

"That was kind of wordy for you," whispered Definimos to Lask.

"I fear that you have rubbed off on me," said Lask into Definimos's ear.

There was more talk among those present, with the Domandosemprians and some Burcs trying to convince the others of the need for necessary military action.

"I have something to say," shouted Rekam. After everyone quieted down, she said, "I may not look like it, but I am your sister. Although those on my planet started out united against tyranny, we had diverse ways of looking at life. We had our difficult times, but we eventually joined in harmony because our roots made us a family, and our goal was to help each other since each individual was precious. Try to keep that goal in mind."

Shouts of agreement filled the space and the Burcs and Domandosemprians pumped their arms in the air as they nodded their respective-sized heads.

"We will do our best to prevent violence," said Definimos. "We must convince those that oppose us that peace and unity are inevitable. However, as you know, we have a challenging time ahead of us."

Everyone there broke down into groups to discuss diplomatic strategies but also to prepare military ones. As those preparations took place, Lask and Definimos pulled Rakam and me aside.

"We feel your work here is done," said Lask. "We must do the rest."

"But, I can give testimony as an objective outsider about what we found in The Safe," I argued. "I have also visited Syntharm and can report on what I witnessed there to show that there can be peace between differing groups."

"We have evidence from The Safe and AM's recordings," said Definimos. "Those who are open to seeing the truth will consider the evidence. Even with Rekam's presence, those who refuse to accept the facts to justify their way of thinking will deny everything and call it all a conspiracy. If we can win over enough individuals, we will prevail."

"And your ship may be used to do great harm," said Lask. "That is why you left your world in the first place."

"We are very grateful for what you have started here, Samuel," said Definimos. "You were the catalyst that brought about this social experiment."

"And a catalyst finishes its task unchanged by leaving the other elements to continue without it," I said, remembering how I thought of my role a while back. "But I hope I have changed. I am trying to, anyway, after my experiences with the both of you, and with Rekam's help."

Rekam and I reached out our hands and joined them. I had sought what was outside of myself and was forging a new way to be.

"I'm not sure I want to return to Earth," I said. "I have enjoyed new, wonderful relationships here with the both of you." I looked at AM who raised his arms as a type of prompt. "And, of course I must not neglect my special connection to AM." AM folded his arms and nodded his head in approval. "And I do know that whatever happens, I will cherish my love for Rekam. I could never hope for a better guide in my personal quests."

"Go back home," urged Lask. "Work to heal your world as you have tried to do with both of ours."

Chapter Forty-Six

The plan was for the Burc/Domandosemprian coalition to engage the Burc drone ships before I took off so that the fighting would create a diversion and allow the Seeker to initiate the HOPS before sustaining an attack. I was to return Rekam to Syntharm so she could inform the inhabitants of what was happening. I dreaded the thought of saying goodbye to Rekam. She anticipated what I was contemplating and had her own ideas.

"I'm coming with you," she said. "I love you and will not let you go without me."

"You can't leave your home and the life there because of me," I said. "It would be unfair to you and your people."

"My people can look after themselves without me," she said. "And, who says I am leaving my home because of you? I am doing it for myself. You have fired the desire in me to explore. And at the same time I will be serving a noble purpose. I can go to Earth and help you with your mission of peace. What a fulfilling opportunity!"

I let out a sigh of relief and had a feeling of happiness unlike any in my life knowing that Rekam would remain with me. We kissed, Syntharmian style, which can take some time, as I previously described. However, I still had to bid farewell to my new friends.

I joined Lask, Definimos, and AM as they readied the assault above the surface of Domandosempria. With the help of cooperating individuals at the airfields, the allied Burcs and Domandosemprians commandeered some of the figure-eight-shaped Domandosemprian crafts and Burc ships that had brought the coalition Burcs to this world.

Definimos handed me an oval-shaped device that had a concave cone on one end and buttons over which the thumb rested at the other end.

"This looks like a weapon," I said. "I don't think I should be bringing back any of your technology to my violence-prone people."

"It is indeed a weapon," said Definimos. "We call it a dissipator. It is a smaller version of those used on our spacecraft and planet that converts matter to liquid and then to gas. Use it to destroy your Seeker when you arrive at your home planet by pressing this red button on the side after aiming the disc at the spacecraft. When that has been accomplished, press both the red and blue buttons simultaneously, throw it up in the air and it will self-destruct."

"We hope that one day we will end all the tools that do harm," said Lask.

I took the dissipator and stored it in my backpack. A feeling of apprehension overwhelmed me.

"I am afraid that you may lose your lives in this battle," I told Lask and Definimos. "I feel like I would be responsible for what could happen to the both of you."

Definimos shook his head and said, "The decision to fight now to secure peace later is ours. You have helped to accelerate the inevitable."

Lask shook his smaller head and said, "He means you made things move fast."

I smiled at my contrasting friends who learned to work together, which allowed me to feel slightly positive about Earth's future.

"I have come to care about both of you very much," I said, my voice almost failing to operate as my emotions took control of the rest of my body.

"And what about me?" asked AM. "I may be a mechanical, but have I not provided you with commendable companionship?"

I laughed and said, "You have been a most excellent comrade, my synthetic friend. May all your circuits remain intact in the days ahead."

"I shall endeavor to accomplish that goal," AM said.

I waved goodbye to them. Rekam and I dodged between buildings, trying to avoid detection by opposing Domandosemprian forces. After getting clear of the city, we reached the spot where I landed the Seeker. We loaded the craft with supplies we carried with us, and then I checked out the Seeker before takeoff.

We waited until the Domandosemprian and Burc ships flew into orbit, giving them time to engage the drones. After securing ourselves, I initiated a takeoff to put the Seeker in a position to break away from the orbit around Domandosempria. Just as we reached the appropriate altitude, there was that dreaded deep vibrating sound nearby that I recognized as the Burc imploder.

"What is that terrible noise?" yelled Rekam.

"Something we do not want to hear up close," I said, and I accelerated my ship out of the line of fire of the Burc weapon. The sonic blast hit another Burc ship instead which throbbed and collapsed into itself. Before I could determine if that was an alliance craft or one of the drones that exploded, I had to continue to evade other Burc ships. Near us several spacecrafts exchanged fire, resulting mostly in near misses. But, some of the vessels either dissipated or imploded. I readied the HOPS to blast out of the attack zone but was worried that Definimos and Lask were on the destroyed ships. Just before I initiated the transducer I received a communication.

"We are still breathing, Samuel." It was the voice of Definimos. I looked at Rekam who appeared as if she was going to cry out of relief.

"I may not be breathing, but I am still here, too," said AM.

"Go in peace," said Lask. "I know that sounds strange while we are at war, but you know what I mean."

"I do," I said as I choked on my relieved words. "Good luck!"

With that, I engaged the HOPS and we rocketed away to the destiny that awaited us.

Part Five

Back Home

Chapter Forty-Seven

We soared to Syntharm and received a relieved welcome from Rekam's people who were happy that we had survived our trip. We told them of the progress that Lask and Definimos had made, and they staged a celebratory feast of thanks to mirror their hope that their relatives would visit them in the near future. The Syntharmians played acoustic musical instruments that had strings and looked like circular guitars. Many danced, sometimes with individuals joining with partners and at other times moving alone.

Rekam told her mother that she was going to Earth with me. She gave her daughter some recent stories she had written to take on the voyage.

"I know you love him," said a smiling Levon. "You must do what you feel is best for you. It sounds like a glorious adventure you are about to embark on."

I was moved by how supportive Levon was and her warmth reminded me of my mother's encouragement as I struggled with my youthful inquisitive mind.

When we took off for Earth, the images I saw this time during the conversion from matter into wave energy were not glorious, but turned out to be, instead, frightening. The visions showed massive explosions, fields of dead bodies, glaciers falling apart and crashing into the sea, cities drowning in tsunamis, and forests and homes igniting in flames. I then felt as if I was flowing through a rapid kaleidoscopic tunnel of colors. As I sped through streams of red, blue, silver-gray, and gold, I heard music from long ago. The end of my favorite Simon and Garfunkel song, "The Boxer," played in my ears. As I hurtled through the twisting colors the vocals and music, punctuated by what sounded like cannons firing, became louder: "Lie la lie/ lie la lie lie lie lie lie lie la la la la lie."

When I regained consciousness I was shaking and sweating. Rekam awoke right after I did and was alarmed by my condition.

"What's the matter?" she asked. "Are you okay?" She held me close to her.

"I'll be fine," I said in a raspy voice. "I saw horrible sights, at least until the end, which was beautiful, but devoid of life. What about you? You seem to have weathered the experience well this time."

I saw that Rekam did not seem upset by her current HOPS experience. In fact, she was smiling.

"The transformation had a different effect on me," she said. "I witnessed the birth of stars and solar systems where creatures rapidly populated the planets and lived together with happy faces as they embraced each other. It was lovely."

I didn't have time to discuss our opposite experiences. The Seeker initiated an alert by way of a beeping alarm as the computer screen displayed that we were approaching Earth. The elapsed time of the flight that we experienced was fifteen minutes and twenty seconds. The speed of my invention was amazing, even to me. I looked through the viewer and saw my quasi-spherical home.

"It looks quite lovely," said Rekam. "Blue and white swirling together."

"You are approaching the planet with a painter's eyes," I said. "I, on the other hand, am experiencing discomfort in another part of my anatomy, the digestive system. It is responding to my anxiety."

I was torn between feeling relief at making it back to Earth safely and the dread of the task ahead of us. I knew that the defense tracking systems would pick up the Seeker's propulsion signature as it reached the atmosphere. I needed to act quickly. I decided to land just outside of Las Vegas, in the desert. I thought it would buy us time to destroy the Seeker but also allow us to hide in the confines of a large city while I attempted to upload my tale onto the major wireless news streams. AM super-compressed the files of my writing onto a digitally integrated contact lens that Definimos gave me. It was an impressive piece of computer interface equipment. By accessing a screen display, I could optically connect with the internet through the visual port of a terminal. I would access the dominant social site, PopFeed, which allowed entries by individuals from all over the world. I wasn't sure how efficiently and quickly the planet's technical service would process this alien program before military intelligence found us. I didn't have a credit app to purchase a personal phone or tablet, so I felt the best way to execute my plan was to log onto PopFeed through a public network at a shared online site.

I landed a few miles from Harry Reid International Airport just outside Vegas. Rekam and I took water and other supplies with us. We stepped onto the sandy cushion of the desolate spot where we landed. We walked a safe distance from the craft, and I pulled the Domandosemprian dissipator out of my backpack. I hesitated.

"You must feel like you are destroying your offspring," said Rekam as she stroked my upper back.

I let out a long sigh. "I put a lot of mental and physical effort into birthing that thing," I said as I pointed the dissipator at the vessel. "I wanted to break boundaries, free us, so that we could learn about existence in this universe. And now I must ghost my creation because unevolved beings will tun it into a monster."

My feeling of loss almost brought tears to my eyes as I aimed the dissipator and fired it at the Seeker. It emitted the familiar piercing white light that engulfed the spacecraft and reduced the Seeker first into a liquid and then a gas that dispersed into the Nevada desert wind. Even though it was gone, I did not have time for mourning since the United States military would soon arrive after tracking us to the landing site. I set the dissipator for self-destruct and tossed it far away from us. It blazed into a smoldering whiteness, transformed into a large bubble of wetness, and then burst into a mushroom of smoke.

"We have to walk to the city," I said. "You better use that hoody I brought from Burc. People may notice your slightly larger forehead even among the inebriated, distracted crowds."

Rekam pulled the hood over her head and we were off.

Chapter Forty-Eight

The sun cooked the sand and cactus plants around us. We drank one quick gulp of liquid every half hour to prevent becoming dried out victims of this desolate land. I tasted the saltiness of perspiration as it dripped down my face and caught it on my tongue in a strange version of recycling water. We first walked for a couple of hours on the crumbly surface but then made it to a two-lane road that headed toward the city. A couple of cars stopped and asked if we needed a ride, but I declined. I didn't want to have to make up some clumsy story about why we were out hiking in this uninhabited area. After two more hours of enduring the desert, we reached the edge of Las Vegas and made our way to the Mandalay Bay Casino and Hotel. There we joined others on trams that took us to the heart of the city. We walked along the sidewalk where there were hordes of people jostling to get to the next show, the next drink, the next bet. After being away from my fellow social beings, I felt disoriented by the crush of so many of my kind. I was beginning to feel like an alien among them.

"What are they all doing here?" asked Rekam in her native tongue which at this point I understood. She had learned English to a sufficient degree, also, and we were in the habit of switching back and forth between languages.

"They are here mostly to gamble, which they could do remotely," I said. "But they enjoy the thrill of playing around others. They get an adrenaline jolt if they win as people envy them for their good luck. If they lose, there are many who they can share their misery with."

People rushed by us, shouting and laughing. Some kissed each other, their hands prowling over the bodies of their desires. Others wore formal evening dress unaware or unconcerned that it was the middle of the day. Electric cars zoomed down the strip showing that the drivers overrode the automated software and raced far above speed limits. A few people slept on park benches, their biological rhythms disrupted, unable to determine the time of day. A few jumped into pools of water near the hotels where lush vegetation grew in contrast to the arid area surrounding the city. There were sidewalk shows featuring simulated earthquakes and tsunamis to amuse the crowds.

"It seems like chaos here," said Rekam as we weaved through the throngs.

"I think that is why people come here," I said. "Let's go in that hotel."

I held Rekam's hand and maneuvered toward the Musk Megagrand Hotel. As we approached the entrance, I heard sirens go off. Long, sleek black jeeps with darkened windows sped toward us and stopped hundreds of feet from our location. From the back of the vehicles soldiers carrying what I recognized as stun rifles emptied out and moved with precision. They came toward the entrance in a V-formation. We ran into the building. I headed for the check-in section, hoping to lose the soldiers in the crowd so I could reach a computer terminal to upload my information. But this military unit was fast and efficient at penetrating the crowd of unaware patrons. They caught us just as I reached my destination. A lieutenant grabbed my arm, and said, "Captain Samuel Galloper, you are under arrest for violating national security."

I was amazed at the speed of the operation. "How did you locate me so quickly?" I asked.

The officer pointed to my left arm and said, "Implant. Admiral Rutlaw had the doctor insert it when she was giving you inoculations. Turned out to be helpful."

Chapter Forty-Nine

The soldiers covered our heads and hustled Rekam and me into one of their vehicles. I heard muted cell phone communications that confirmed that our capture was successful. The fact that they apprehended two of us seemed to elicit surprise from what I could discern. We rode along for quite a while. Rekam leaned over to me and said, "Your people are not very hospitable."

Before I could say anything, a soldier yelled, "Shut up and be still!"

"And lack a sense of humor," Rekam said in a whisper.

After what seemed like at least an hour the vehicle stopped. Our captors pulled us out of the jeep and propelled us forward. I heard sliding doors and assumed we were inside a building now as the outside sound of wind rushing by receded. Then there was the whooshing sound of another door opening and our captors pushed us to the left. Someone shoved me into a chair and removed my hood. A female soldier then took the hood off the seated Rekam. We were in a small, dimly lit room with two armed soldiers staring at us.

"Well, looky here," said the male soldier with a smile. "This woman looks like she is either going to COMICON or has had some plastic surgery."

The female soldier shook her head and said, "Try not to act like your idiotic self, will ya.' She's an alien, you fool. Galloper here brought her back after being in outer space."

"She's an illegal alien then," said the male, chuckling. "I'll shoot her so she can't get my job."

Before the woman could insult her comrade once more, the door behind them slid open and I saw a familiar face I never wanted to set eyes on again.

"Welcome back to Earth, Galloper," said Admiral Rutlaw. "You're not getting away this time. And neither is your friend."

Chapter Fifty

"Do you want to see the people you care about?" was Admiral Rutlaw's rhetorical question. "Then you better cooperate this time. We have everything you need here, just like before. Let's make it easier the second time around."

Déjà vu all over again, I said to myself. After extracting us from the secure site in Nevada, guards took us to a military transport airplane and flew us east. Now, inside the large high-tech room in which I found myself, I looked around and it was as if Rutlaw had frozen my lab in time, like nothing had changed. I was back at the NASA base in Florida with guards stationed outside the room that I could see through the crisscrossed metal mesh embedded in the glass door window. The holographic simulators were present which could virtually create the effects that my theoretical research predicted. There were several state-of-the-art 3-D printers that I would need to create my propulsion components. And outside I knew there were engineers that could construct the finished product that would house the completed parts.

"Are you a soldier or a jailer?" I said, expressing my own rhetorical comment.

Rutlaw inhaled deeply and his face inflated like a helium balloon in a parade. "I have been, am, and will always be a soldier before anything else," he said. "Whatever I do, it is because of my loyalty to the great nation I am proud to serve." He then brought his face with the Kirk Douglas jaw close to mine and added, "And I will do whatever it takes to defeat my country's enemies."

"Back off," I said. "I can smell your taco lunch. Where is Rekam?"

Rutlaw smiled and walked behind the chair where I sat. "You mean the alien you brought here," he said. "Who knows what type of infestation she might have that could ravage our world. That's why we had to put you and her through the anticontamination procedures. How could you debase your humanity by attaching yourself to that creature?"

"She shows more humanity in a minute than you could ever hope to achieve in a lifetime," I shot back. "What have you done to her?"

"She's in isolation for now. Our doctors are making sure we didn't miss anything, and that she isn't a carrier of something that can harm us," Rutlaw said.

"If you even think about harming her ..." I started.

"Enough of this insubordination!" he said. "Let's get down to brass tacks, as my father used to say. If you want to see your alien and your brother again, you will recreate your project. This time, there will be no escape. Think about that and I'll come back for your answer."

Rutlaw then marched out of the room, leaving me alone with my conflicting thoughts. I paced around the lab that doubled for my cell and agonized about what results my actions would produce. I desperately wanted to see Rekam. My heart pounded and my head throbbed as I wondered what Rutlaw had in store for her. But, if I agreed to recreate my work, the military could use my invention to devastate others through the rapid transport of soldiers and weapons. Rutlaw's scientists might learn how to reverse the HOPS effect. I did not inform Rutlaw of that outcome, as I mentioned earlier. Reducing matter to various states of density, even to the point of creating a vortex of immense gravity, could result in mass devastation. How could I be responsible for such apocalyptic results?

I also worried that Rutlaw might use the threat of harming Arthur as leverage against me. I concluded that I must get my story out to produce public outrage against the abuse of my invention. To do that I had to pretend to go along with Rutlaw while attempting to delay progress on my scientific activities. I had to pass my recorded story on the digital contact lens to Arthur so he could find a way to disseminate my tale.

I gambled that Rutlaw could not suspect my plan and I hoped he would think my actions were not a threat.

"I want to see Rekam on a daily basis," I told Rutlaw, "as well as my brother."

"As long as you hold up your end of the bargain, that can be arranged," said Rutlaw.

"If you harm either of them, the deal is off," I said.

"That works for me," said Rutlaw. "But we will monitor you, so speak in English. This is America, after all. You will not discuss details of your travels with your brother. That's classified information and we don't want any press snooping around here."

"Yeah, don't want the Constitution to spoil your plans," I said, trying to put as much contempt as I could into my words.

Rutlaw ignored my comment and said, "You can talk about how your brother is doing and he can update you on what you've missed while away. Your brother will have a guard with him day and night to ensure secrecy about your being here and our work."

"You mean my work, don't you?" I said.

Rutlaw just smiled, revealing his oversized teeth.

Chapter Fifty-One

I dragged my scientific feet, slowly setting up files that consisted of background data, studies concerning exotic matter, and computations about extracting energy from photons. Rutlaw did allow Arthur to see me.

"Your smile tells me you are relieved," I said to him.

"Of course I am," Arthur said. "I thought I was never going to see you again. But your eyes are squinting. You look tired. I assume you haven't been sleeping."

"I have been working long days and could use enough rest for two people," I said and raised my eyebrows. Arthur returned the facial movement. Since the time we were children, my brother and I loved playing charades. We even made up our own code of body movements and later verbal expressions to convey messages. Athur's response here meant that he understood that I was not alone in my predicament and that Rutlaw was forcing me to labor for him.

Arthur asked me if I was healthy after whatever journey I had undertaken, and I assured him that physically (purposefully excluding mentally) I was doing well enough. We talked about his writing.

"I'm working on a story about two brothers who choose different paths of life but then come together in the end," said Arthur.

"Sounds familiar," I said with a smile. "I have an idea for a dystopian novel about a world that appears free and happy on the surface but which has monsters controlling everything from underground."

Arthur winked at me, letting me know he understood and said, "I think that has been done before. *The Time Machine* comes to mind."

"There's always another variation on the tale," I said.

***

Rutlaw delivered Rekam to me as promised. She looked thinner and the dark skin under her eyes revealed a lack of sleep. I noticed several needle marks on her arms. But she smiled broadly when she saw me, embraced me with a firm hug, and gave me a passionate kiss, only on the lips this time.

"I have missed you so!" she said in English, looking into my eyes and then focusing on the so far hidden contact lens on the right. I gave a quick shake of my head to break her focus.

"How have they treated you?" I asked while keeping her in my arms.

"They have asked me many questions, mostly about weapons I might know about," she said. "I told them I am an artist, not a soldier, but they insanely kept asking the same thing over and over, expecting me to say something else." She added loudly, "And, I must say the food and drink in this place has been minimal and unappetizing."

"Do you have any blood left?" I asked, pointing to the needle marks.

"I remember reading about vampires in your literary library," said Rekam. "Apparently they are not just fictional."

I held her tighter and kissed her again.

"How are things going?" she said, and I knew she was asking about my plans to get the information out.

"I'm sure progress will speed up soon," I said. "Oh, and I will be meeting with Arthur again tomorrow."

"I know you have told me how concerned your brother was about your mental state before your voyages," Rekam said. "What will you tell him about what you have learned and how you are doing now after your travels?"

I thought about Burc and the desire for a secure, regimented life, and the rule-breaking existence on Domandosempria. I looked at Rekam and remembered the joy on Syntharm where the inhabitants lived in peace and experienced fulfillment through artistic expression.

"Arthur knows all too well how torn I always have been between wanting to know everything, questioning everything," I said, "and yearning for a sanctuary, which I partially found in the military. I suppose we all exist on that spectrum to one degree or another, and possibly slide back and forth depending on the circumstances at any given time. We strive for the infinite but are not really capable of grasping it. Then we retreat to the security of our retaining walls."

"Making sense of the universe is a need for self-conscious creatures," said Rekam. "So, where do you go from here?" Rekam asked.

"I suppose I hope to be able to continue to write," I said.

Chapter Fifty-Two

Notes About the Second Edition

As I write this addendum in the den in my house situated in Maryland, eighteen months have passed since I was able to get my story to Arthur. I included additional material in my log after my abduction, including the letter to the publisher, for a time without my jailers learning my intentions by speaking out loud in Syntharmian so the contact lens could record my words. AM installed a nano translation program on the optical device to make my words accessible to those who spoke other languages on Earth. Rutlaw questioned me about what I had been saying in an unknown foreign language.

"It is poetry that I learned on my travels. It comforts me," I said. He demanded that I only speak in English afterwards, so from that point forward I was only able to record raw dialogue for the first edition.

At our second meeting while I was under Rutlaw's surveillance, I joked with Arthur about how in the future it would be remarkable if a writer could transmit his or her manuscript by looking at an optical scanner on a computer screen. While we laughed about how strange that might be, I slipped him the digital recording lens. Of course, at the time that this happened, I didn't know if others would ever read what I wrote. My brother is actually the smarter sibling in many ways and figured out what was going on. Since Arthur was under continual surveillance he was not able to transmit any comments or information to streaming news sources or social media sites concerning my travels and current imprisonment. However, in a video session with his publisher where he submitted the first draft of his new novel for editing, Arthur wore the lens and transmitted my files.

I am grateful that the first edition was a huge success as my story accompanied by the visuals from my recording device went viral. If you have followed what transpired after the publication, you know that the public outcry against what Admiral Rutlaw was doing led to my release, along with that of my now wife, Rekam. At least that is what I consider her to be. Her citizenship on Earth is a complicated matter. We had a civil ceremony which seems to have been accepted by the population in general. After my release, I was able to rewrite my story in more detail and with my impressions about what transpired after our capture in Las Vegas. I worked with Arthur and several editors to refine the writing and bring you the version of the story you have before you in this second edition.

Rekam and I live in privacy, but not seclusion. Arthur visits us often from his home in Towson. We enjoy giving talks (Rekam has learned several of Earth's languages) in person and online about our experiences. I hope some of you have attended the live presentations, or will be able to in the future. Rekam has continued her painting and has produced works illustrating the mountains, pastures and streams of her misty home planet. They have been featured in art galleries in New York and Chicago and on numerous internet sites. I have continued writing and am working on a science fiction novel so I can explore the nature of existence in fiction.

I also yearn to see Lask, Definimos, and, of course, AM once more. There is never an end to inquiry, since one question always leads to another, as I noted before. But, the arts give communal form to what we all puzzle over. Art tries to shine a creative light so people can perceive their reality with greater perception. And, of course, love expands us beyond our finite selves and joins us all to each other and to the infinite beyond. To help others find a degree of mental peace is the best one can do. How much of my story feels real? Like all tales, to one degree or another, it is derived from a true story.

Rekam and I hope that our lives and the examples of Burc, Domandosempria, and Syntharm might offer possibilities for an insightful and happier future.

* 9 7 9 8 2 3 0 6 0 2 4 2 2 *